CLOVELLY

Frederick Faust
(Max Brand)

Alias the Night Wind

BY VARICK VANARDY

*The Blue Fire Pearl: The Complete Adventures
of Singapore Sammy, Volume 1*

BY GEORGE F. WORTS

Drink We Deep

BY ARTHUR LEO ZAGAT

The Gun-Brand

BY JAMES B. HENDRYX

Jan of the Jungle

BY OTIS ADELBERT KLINE

Minions of the Moon

BY WILLIAM GREY BEYER

The Moon Pool & The Conquest of the Moon Pool

BY ABRAHAM MERRITT

Tarzan and the Jewels of Opar

BY EDGAR RICE BURROUGHS

*War Lord of Many Swordsmen:
The Adventures of Norcross, Volume 1*

BY W. WIRT

CLOVELLY

MAX BRAND

COVER BY

PAUL STAHR

ALTUS PRESS
2017

© 2017 Steeger Properties, LLC, under license to Altus Press • First Edition—2017

EDITED AND DESIGNED BY
Matthew Moring

PUBLISHING HISTORY
"Clovelly" originally appeared in the September 27, October 4, 11, 18 and 25, and November 1, 1924 issues of *Argosy All-Story Weekly* magazine (Vol. 163, No. 3–Vol. 164, No. 2). Copyright © 1924 by The Frank A. Munsey Company. Copyright renewed © 1951 and assigned to the Frederick Faust Trust. All rights reserved. Images copyright © 1924 by The Frank A. Munsey Company. Copyright renewed © 1951 and assigned to Steeger Properties, LLC. All rights reserved.
"About the Author" originally appeared in the December 10, 1932 issue of *Argosy* magazine (Vol. 234, No. 5). Copyright © 1932 by The Frank A. Munsey Company. Copyright renewed © 1960 and assigned to Steeger Properties, LLC. All rights reserved.

THANKS TO
Everard P. Digges LaTouche and Gerd Pircher

ISBN
978-1-61827-301-7

Visit *altuspress.com* for more books like this.
Printed in the United States of America.

TABLE OF CONTENTS

CHAPTER I

THE GAMECOCK'S SPUR

THOSE IN THIS London street who looked up to the oriel window admired the gracefulness of the stone scrollwork which bracketed it out from the wall, and the slenderness of the mullions that supported the little squares of leaded glass and arose to a tangle of intricate tracery at the top. Indeed, the window, with the rich red of the curtain which screened the interior of the room, had an air of half Moorish enchantment. And it was a day as fair as any that ever arched over far-off Granada. It was such a day as made men forget the mud in the street and look up to the smoke-blackened fronts of the buildings, seeing pleasant and gay details like this oriel window for the first time, perhaps, and then staring higher to the unaccustomed blue of the sky.

For though London is dim nowadays, it was a dark, dark city in that time when the Merry Monarch was but newly seated upon the throne of his father. The houses were huddled one upon another like frightened sheep, and from a close-crammed myriad of chimneys the smoke of the sea-coal rolled steadily up and was woven into the warp of the fog which rarely left the sky, and together with it drew a close gray veil across the city.

But this day a wind came clipping briskly over the land with the fresh purity of spring fields, and the sweetness of flowers in its breath; it tossed the sea mist back to the sea; it scoured the coal smoke out of the air; and London, looking up into the

1

sparkling blue, could have exclaimed with one voice: "There is a heaven above us, after all!"

In a trice the pens of poets were scratching frantically, the brushes of painters were swashing the colors upon the canvas, and the trembling musicians were trying to make the glory of that day pass into their instruments. But still wiser were those who made no effort to capture this rare day, but who went out to spend its beauty as fast as it came pouring down.

Of the sensible ones was Michael Clovelly, for he had drawn his sword belt a notch tighter about his empty belly, paid for his night's lodging with his last coppers, and now wandered through the streets with a blithe hope that good fortune might be lying in wait for him around any corner. And, when he passed that oriel window and saw the darkly handsome young man who stared gloomily out from behind it, he could not help taking off his hat and waving it so that the wind flaunted the red feather that curled upon its brim.

So doing, his eye was raised from the drift of people about him, and the next instant he was shouldered so heavily to the side that one boot sank deep in the kennel. For in those days pavements were little known in London.

The footpath on either side was set off from the street by long rows of posts, and between the footpath and the street there was a deep gutter called the kennel, in which the rain water and the slops thrown from the windows of the houses flowed sluggishly. To keep the wall was a necessity if one wished to retain clean feet.

The temper of Michael Clovelly was as peaceful as well-dried gunpowder. Now he shook the filth from his boot, and wheeled about to see a towering fellow who passed on shaking his wide shoulders with laughter and cocking up the end of his long rapier beneath his cloak.

A passing apprentice had stopped his cry of "What d'ye lack?" and paused to laugh also; but the next instant he was crowing "Fight! Fight!" like a little rooster to gather a crowd to

see the fun, for Michael Clovelly had stepped up to the big man and twitched his cloak.

The jostler wheeled with such violence that his cloak flared as wide as a vulture's wings, and, scowling down at Clovelly, he clapped a hand upon the hilt of his heavy rapier.

"What will you have?" he roared.

"Your apology," answered Clovelly, "or your blood, you fat-gutted bullock!"

The voice of the other exploded in inarticulate joy at the thought of battle. A dexterous motion of his left arm twitched the cloak from his shoulders and coiled it in thick folds around his forearm, and at the same instant he swished the long blade from the scabbard and with the single motion flicked the point at the pace of the smaller man.

Only a backward leap saved his nose from being slashed across; then his own weapon winked out of its sheath, and he stood on guard, measuring his work. It seemed a very great work indeed!

He was himself of no more than the middle height and very sparely made. In the wide shoulders of the other there was twice his bulk and several inches advantage in reach. That was not all. Their weapons were as mismated as their persons, for Clovelly carried a small-sword with a triangular blade tapering smoothly from fort through foible to a long needle point. It was a new fashion in blades, lately introduced in France, but still a great novelty for England.

The rapier of the big man, on the other hand, was one of those tremendous cut-and-thrust weapons which had an edge capable of shearing through armor and far more than a yard of steel from hilt to point.

And their methods of attack and defense were as different as their weapons or their persons. The big man rushed in and poured a storm of steel at his antagonist, sweeping cuts which might almost have shorn the head from his shoulders, great lunges, mezzo-drittos at the wrist, rovescios at the knee of Clovelly.

At the same time he weaved back and forth, passing to the right so that he swung in a great circle on which Clovelly was more or less the center. For defense he had not only his blade for parrying, but the cloak which was wrapped about his left arm.

And yet, quite mysteriously, Clovelly did not go down bathed in gore. His left arm he flung idly behind him; his right he kept well extended with the point more or less steadily threatening the throat and breast of the other.

At the same time, with the base of his triangular blade, he picked off the attacks of the other, clicking the thrusts and the lunges sharply away and making the cuts slither harmlessly off the steel. As for his footwork, it consisted in dancing lightly in and out and never to the side.

The whole affair took hardly thirty seconds, but it was time enough for the spectators who had paused and turned to watch or rushed to windows or out of doors, to stop holding their breath in expectation of the slaughter of the smaller man and to shout in admiration of his wonderful address. For twenty-nine seconds he did nothing but defend.

Then he stepped in, his rapier's point darted out like a snake's tongue, and the big fellow dropped his weapon, yelling an oath.

He had been pricked in the wrist.

The fallen sword Clovelly kicked into the kennel, and while the other floundered after it he had sheathed his own blade, turned upon his heel, and went jauntily on his way, hardly breathing from the exercise. He was given a cheer. The bully received a laugh and a few stinging words as he slouched away; and then the tide of life in the street flowed on exactly as before. But a change of fortune was waiting for Clovelly. He had turned a corner a little later when a hand tapped his shoulder and he swung around to find a youth confronting him quite out of breath from the speed with which he had been running and only able to gasp out:

"My Lord Teynham—my lord—my Lord Teynham—"

"Well," said Clovelly, "if he's your lord, he's wasted a devilish deal of money fitting you out in these clothes. Are you in the service of Lord Teynham?"

For the lad was dressed in brilliant, plum-colored velvet jacket and breeches with rich lace dangling about his wrists and over the backs of his hands, and a fine lace collar blowing about his shoulders. He was bareheaded, to attest the speed with which he had darted out upon his mission, and his long, curling hair had been tossed into disorder.

He was as slenderly made as a girl, as fine of hand and foot, and there was more of the feminine than the masculine about the beauty of his face—except that all was made wholly boyish by an eye as frank, as bold, and as impishly wise as ever looked out of an English face.

"I'm in his service," said the boy, "and damn me if I've ever done a harder bit than to catch you. You walk with seven-league boots, sir! I am to bring you back with me at once."

With this he turned upon his heel and gestured to Clovelly to follow. But Michael was in no hurry; he was scenting an adventure and perhaps a meal in the near future, and he ached to go after the youngster; yet he had a certain uncomfortable pride of person which had to be consulted at every twist and turning of his life. It rooted him now in his place.

"Your pockets," he said, "seem a bit small for me. How are you to take me back to Lord Teynham?"

The youngster turned in surprise and looked Clovelly over from head to foot, but he appeared to find nothing in the worn clothes and the muddy boots of the man to explain this attitude.

"Do you know who Lord Teynham is?" he asked.

"I never heard the name till now."

The boy frowned, changed his mind, and grinned broadly.

"Well," he said, "if my lord were to hear that, he'd be the most surprised man in England. He would lay you a florin to a groat that there is not a man in England past six years old who has not heard of Francis Willenden, my Lord Teynham!"

"And what the devil has my Lord Teynham done," asked Clovelly, "that every man in England should know him? I have been out of the kingdom for a few years. Tell me the distinctions of his lordship."

"Why," replied the boy, "he has done all manner of great things and he's barely turned twenty-five."

"As young as that!" remarked Clovelly, who was himself exactly that age. "A mere youngster—but what has he done?"

"He won the great match race last year from his grace of Ipswich and five thousand guineas."

He waited; and when Clovelly smiled, he grinned as well.

"He has been sent to Paris in an embassy and come back with the hearts of a dozen Paris beauties."

"Wonderful!" exclaimed Clovelly, still smiling.

"And Old Rowley himself asks Teynham's advice on matters of dress."

"If his majesty himself consults him about such an important affair," said Clovelly, "I see that he is indeed a great man."

"His lordship will agree with you," declared the imp. "Are you persuaded to come with me now?"

"I am not persuaded—I am commanded," Clovelly admitted. "Lead on; and I follow."

And they turned back together down the same street up which Clovelly had just come.

CHAPTER II

WRIST OF STEEL

THE DOOR THEY entered was under that very oriel window which Clovelly had noticed before; and presently he was ushered into a room where there paced up and down the same handsome, dark-faced youth whom he had seen sitting in gloomy mien at the window. The page, who had learned the name of his companion as they climbed the stairs, presented him duly and then disappeared through the doorway. His lordship waved his visitor to a chair, but continued himself to pace up and down the room, scowling, and apparently at a loss for a way in which to open the conversation. But at length he turned and said:

"You have been in France, I see?"

Clovelly nodded.

"I sat at this window and saw you make a fool of that tall brawler. It was neat work. I have seen some famous blades, but that was very neat work."

"You are kind," Clovelly returned, and let his eye rove. He could smell cookery somewhere in the house, and the fragrance filled him with a sense of weakness. It was a handsomely furnished apartment, from the oil portrait of an old cavalier in the armor of 1640 to the stiff tapestry which hung upon the other side of the room. His lordship was the brightest note in the chamber, however, for he was clad in a crimson dressing gown heavily brocaded in both silver and gold, and the lining, where the robe hung open, was of the richest green silk. He was not yet dressed for the street, for it was hardly noon, and at such an early hour no gentleman of fashion, of course, dared to show himself.

Green slippers with red heels were upon his feet; a chain of gold mesh clasped against one wrist what might have been an incased miniature. About his shoulders descended his long black hair in the most carefully ordered curls. And his face was as vain and haughty as that of a feminine beauty.

"So much for the sword-play which caught my eye. And there was something in your guard—that slight bend in the arm—which suggested Italy. Have you studied in that country also?"

"I have been in Italy," admitted Clovelly.

"And yet you had method, too, and a certain confidence which I have never seen except in the Spanish masters. Mr. Clovelly, I wonder if you have not traveled in Spain also?"

"I have had the privilege of watching the great Rivernol in his school at Cordova."

"Ah!" cried his lordship. "You have been around the world in great part learning the tricks of the sword!"

"I have been around the world in great part," said Clovelly, "but as for tricks, I hold them not worthy an empty nutshell."

His lordship frowned.

"That is a round, bold speech," he declared. "We have many masters in London, and there is not one that does not teach more tricks than method. What is your secret to develop skill with the sword?"

Clovelly looked thoughtfully before him for a moment. Then he drew his smallsword softly from its sheath and held it with his arm stretched out full length and the blade horizontal.

"When I see a man who can do this," he explained, "I shall fear him more than all the tricksters in the world. I have heard these grave professors make a mystery out of fencing; but I have learned to laugh at them."

My Lord Teynham was plainly taken aback, but though he was about to scoff away the suggestion of Clovelly, yet the manner of the latter was so frank and his air so easy and so confident that his lordship hesitated.

"Upon my honor," he objected, "I see nothing in what you are doing."

"There is a silver knife on that table. Do with it as I am doing."

His lordship scooped up the knife and held it forth.

"There," he said. "And what of it? Is this a jest, sir?"

"The knife trembles, my lord. The light shakes on it."

"So, then—"

He centered his mind and his nerve upon the task.

"The light still quivers on that metal, sir."

His lordship tossed the knife away and stared again at the rapier in the hand of his guest. It had been extended in a trying position for some minutes now, but it stood as stiff as if it were fixed in the solid wall and not in a hand of flesh and bone. Clovelly now put up his weapon.

"A very clever trick," admitted my lord.

"No trick, if you please."

"How is it managed, then?"

"Most simply. An hour in the morning and an hour in the afternoon of work with the sword and exercises to strengthen the wrist, and this done for five years at least, will make you the master of a steady sword, my lord."

His lordship shrugged his shoulders and a ripple of gold light and of silver fled up and down the robe which clothed him.

"I can almost believe it," he conceded, smiling. "But after all, what is the use of this steadiness, most amazing though it is?"

"Have you seen time-thrusts and stop-thrusts used?"

"By the score, of course."

"And most of them failures?"

"That is true; for they must be brought off in the precise part of a second which is intended, and the sword must travel as true as a plumb line. Otherwise, they are disastrous."

"Very good, then. And the only man who truly knows where the point of his sword is going is he who knows that the pommel is firm as a rock in his hand."

Clovelly sighed and shook his head.

"How many times," he continued, "a thrust has gone clean home, but has passed through nothing but the clothes of a man while the hilt rapped against his ribs; how many a sword point has slid past the cheek instead of through the eye at which it was aimed!

"Oh, my lord, a man will tell you that accuracy is indeed a most necessary thing with his pistol, but for his sword-play he seems to forget that a miss of half an inch may be as good as a miss of a yard. Besides, he who knows just where the point will go need not overreach himself and try to drive his blade clean through the body when two short inches may be enough to touch the heart."

His lordship listened with a peculiar interest, as indeed every gentleman or boor of that day would have listened to a novel view concerning the use of weapons. For the sword which accompanied the dandy in his walk had to be a useful tool as well as an ornament, and the code which every gentleman learned was that certain offenses could only be pardoned or punished with the sword.

"All this," said his lordship, "may be true. But a duel is fought at close hand; the weapon is small, the target is large, and surely it seems to me that even a child could understand that what is most needed is speed in the parry and lightning quickness of foot and hand for the lunge and thrust. Speed, surely, is the prime necessity."

"A swift hand," said Clovelly—and his voice lowered to an almost religious awe—"is truly the gift of God made more precious still by practice which never relents. The hand moves, and the eye cannot follow—"

He illustrated with a lightning gesture. His hand seemed to disappear upon one side of his chair and came into being again resting upon the other arm. His lordship said nothing, but so keen was his interest that he appeared to have forgotten all that had first been burdening his mind.

"A swift hand—and a swift foot hardly less—is indeed a precious thing, without which nothing may be done. But there lies my point: that the swiftest hand need not always win; the sure hand is better still."

"I cannot agree, Mr. Clovelly."

"Consider," argued the other, "that to the man who is not absolutely sure of his mark the target is restricted. If a man aims for the head, he dares not thrust save at the very center of the face, for fear that he will miss entirely. He dares not aim at the corners, which are twenty times open to attack whereas the center is only open once.

"He cannot slip his point through a cheek and madden his man with the pain of it and the thought of disfiguration. He cannot flick his point across a forehead and blind his man with blood, or snip the point, again, across the very tip of the nose, which will cloud even the eyes of a hero with tears and so start him fighting in a fog.

"Or, again, he fears to aim at such a small and shifting target as a wrist or an elbow, a knee, or a hundred places where a fencer may be so stung as to cripple him for the one vital instant, or else turn him blind with passion.

"I tell you finally, my lord, that a man who is not sure of his point has to fight to kill and so many a murder is done, but he who knows where the point will strike and where it will end to the width of a hair and to the thickness of a sheet of paper holds his enemy at his mercy on the one hand and spares his life with the other."

He arose as he spoke, his color mounting, his brown eyes shining, while his lordship watched and listened with a growing awe. He noted now that, upon a closer scrutiny, Mr. Clovelly seemed less fragile than before. He was lean, to be sure, but so is the hunting leopard.

And as Michael Clovelly stepped out from the shadow into the sunny end of the room, it was to be seen that his hair was not the mere brown which it had appeared before, but a lustrous black that suddenly gave a certain character and ominous distinction to his thin face and to the darkness of his eyes. He now was picking from the table a plate of Chinese porcelain, very thin and composed of the most intricate interweaving of fragile threads of gilt and enamel.

It was an age in which a passion for Chinese porcelains crammed every fashionable household with grinning, glistening dragons and wildly designed vases, but even in that time this plate—or, rather, shallow basket—was as unusual as it was precious and beautiful. Clovelly now held it to the light and pointed out his object to Lord Teynham. In the exact center there was a very small hole, and this Clovelly indicated.

"Consider, my lord, if this is not worth some dozen of the tricks of the fencing masters."

With this, he spun the plate high in the air, brought his rapier hissing from its scabbard, and thrust. The whole movement was so quick that the sword turned into a ray of light.

But the plate of porcelain was held fast on the end of that narrow beam and Clovelly presented it to the master of the house. The point of the weapon had passed not more than a few inches through the aperture.

Lord Teynham removed the porcelain and replaced it thoughtfully upon the table. He remained for a time in deep thought without speaking a word.

"You are a dangerous fellow, Clovelly," he declared at length, "and after what I have seen to-day alone I should be confident in you against very great masters indeed. All of which makes me feel that you are sent me from heaven in my time of need."

He fastened a keen eye on the other, but Clovelly had resumed his place in his chair and endured the scrutiny with the greatest calm; for his whole manner in this exhibition had not been that of one who makes a vain display and endeavors to win applause. It was rather that of one who seriously and eagerly supports a theory and having demonstrated his point has no further personal pride in the matter.

"As for that, my lord," he replied, "I presume it depends upon what your need may be. But if it is a thing that may be done by a man of honor," he continued with a peculiar emphasis, "I am at your service."

CHAPTER III

A NOVICE HIGHWAYMAN

HIS LORDSHIP WAS young and intense, but he was also not without a sense of humor, and his eyes were glinting as he looked steadily at Clovelly. "It seems to me," he said, "that there is something left out of your statement; which is: What will a hungry man do for food?"

Clovelly stood not upon his dignity, but grinned in turn. On this clew his lordship continued: "A private coach is starting on the Oxford Road this afternoon. I want that coach stopped and something taken from it."

Clovelly rubbed his chin.

"I saw the hanging at Tyburn yesterday," he remarked, "where Captain Vincent, the highwayman, was strung up."

His lordship nodded.

"To a man who has fear, of course, what I ask is impossible."

"You, my lord," said Clovelly, "seem a man of courage."

"I hope I have my share, but I am not hungry."

"Very true. I am to commit highway robbery, then, for the sake of a full belly."

"And certain pounds."

Clovelly considered for an instant.

"I might as well be frank. I had as soon take this work for the sake of the adventure as well as the money that may be in it. To be a highwayman by voluntary choice I should consider as an act of horror and disgrace; but to be a highwayman by request, my lord, is quite another matter."

His lordship was greatly pleased, for he began to nod and smile more broadly than ever.

"Can you mount yourself and arm yourself within the hour?"

"With money."

"Here is forty pounds. Is it enough?"

"Double the amount I need," Clovelly asserted, but he calmly pocketed the sum.

His lordship frowned, but straightway was smiling again.

"This is a disreputable business," he said, "and if you were to make off with that money, I should have no way of bringing you to account for it. However," he added, "I trust you, Mr. Clovelly."

The other thanked him with a graceful inclination of his head.

"Remember," cautioned Lord Teynham, "that the price of a good horse comes uncommonly high this year."

"I know the one I shall take."

"And the price of it?"

"It is pulling a peddler's cart," said Clovelly. "I saw it yesterday, and from the look of the driver I imagine the price will be small enough."

"And for pistols?"

"This will serve my purpose, I presume."

And straightway he reached into the breasts of his threadbare coat and brought deftly forth two long barreled weapons so cared for and polished that they shone like silver. The butts were rubbed black with long handling, and the guns balanced lightly in his slender hands. Lord Teynham had started from his chair at the sudden sight of such an armament.

"In the name of heaven!" he exclaimed, "Do you carry such an outfit with you, weighing you down, every day? And how by all that is mysterious can you carry such guns in your clothes?"

"It is a habit," Clovelly explained, "which I formed in Turkey, where it is often wise to carry pistols—but not so wise, at times, to let them be seen. As for their bulk, you see that they are extraordinarily slender."

In fact, at a closer examination, his lordship discovered that they were small indeed.

"They will carry a bullet hardly larger than a pea!" he cried.

"But heavier," said Clovelly. "And with a good charge of powder behind them, they will pierce a thickness of wood that would surprise you, to say nothing of mere flesh. As for the size of the ball, there again let me suggest that it is not how heavily a man is struck with a bullet but where the bullet lands. Do we need to blow away half of a man's leg to stop him? Or tear his head to bits to kill him?"

"By heaven," his lordship remarked, leaning still closer, "they are most exquisitely overlaid with gold cashing. I wonder that you would go hungry rather than part with at least one of them for a price."

Clovelly restored his guns to their hiding places with a single gesture.

"They were gifts from one whose memory I prize very dearly," he said, shortly. "And now, my lord, for the business on hand."

His lordship still stared with something of the hungry curiosity of a child at Clovelly's coat which appeared in no wise fattened in any place or bulging because of the implements which had been placed inside it; on the contrary, the form of the man was in appearance as gaunt as ever.

"That business," he said, "means a vast deal to me. You will imagine that when I pick a man off the street to work for me."

"I wonder at it," murmured Clovelly.

"Because," his lordship went on, "though I could hire a dozen rough blades to attempt this thing, and though perhaps they might carry it through to the end well enough, how could I be sure that they would not use blackmail afterward and so bleed me white? In a word, Clovelly, I can be served in this only by a man of some honor."

Clovelly waved his hand, as if so much were to be taken for granted.

"As for the work itself, the coach is that of Sir Christopher Redbourne. Lady Redbourne travels with him. And in particular, they are accompanied by young Herbert Theale, the viscount of Pennistone. They take the Oxford road and turn off on the Pennistone road, bound for the manor of that name.

"Clovelly, that coach must be stopped, and from the person of young Theale must be taken a certain locket which contains the picture of a young lady of great beauty. That you may recognize the picture, I may tell you that she has hair of pale gold, with blue eyes and very finely drawn, high-arched brows. It is an excellent bit of painting in the small. You cannot fail but recognize it when it is seen."

Clovelly said not a word.

"As for her name," continued Lord Teynham, blushing in spite of himself, "that is, of course, not to be known, either now or hereafter."

"Naturally."

"There will be in the coach other things of far greater value—to you!—than this locket. By all means help yourself and re-munerate yourself for the work, Besides which, if you succeed in this adventure I shall give you—"

He hesitated, his lips drawn thin, his eyes boring at the face of Clovelly, as if he hoped to penetrate to the very soul of that young man.

"If I succeed," Clovelly interposed, with a touch of scorn in his voice, "I shall have been paid by the airing in the country roads, by the forty pounds which you have so generously given me, and by the horse which shall be between my legs when I return."

His lordship sprang to his feet and waved unceremoniously toward the door.

"Then start at once in the name of God! They may take the

road early; they may take the road late. Perhaps they may not start until the evening of this warm day."

"They have no fear of robbers, then, if they ride by night."

"God bless us, in these rough days it seems to make but a small difference if men travel either by night or by day, for these ruffianly highway robbers had as soon take a purse by high noon as by full moon, and as soon by the moonlight as in the dark."

"With how large an escort does Sir Christopher usually ride?"

His lordship bit his lip, as if this were a question which he would gladly have left unanswered, depending upon his man to go through the business, once committed to it, no matter how difficult it might prove.

"A small matter," he answered. "There will be the coachman and a footman beside him in the seat, of course. But fellows of that cloth are a mere nothing to a man of determination."

Clovelly had folded his hands and awaited the recital with an air which was neither indifferent nor excited.

"There will be an outrider or two, and I take it that this will be all."

"A brace of men who ride before the carriage," summed up Michael Clovelly calmly, "and two more on the seat, and two gentlemen inside the coach, to say nothing of another pair who may be riding in the rear. In all, six men certainly, and perhaps eight; and I am to stop this coach, my lord?"

His lordship scowled at the floor.

"In the name of the devil," he groaned, "am I to hire a whole brigade of—"

"Of cutthroats?" finished Clovelly. "By no means!"

He arose from his chair.

"You'll go through with it, Clovelly?" asked Lord Teynham, clutching his hands together in his anxiety. "Or else I'm a ruined man!"

The last phrase broke involuntarily from his lips, but Clovelly nodded.

"As you said before, an empty belly is an eloquent advocate to advise desperate deeds, Sir. And when must I be back?"

"By midnight at the very latest. By midnight. I shall be in an agony!"

"Fifty miles of riding, a coach to be found and stopped, and all by midnight? Farewell, my lord," said Clovelly, and swiftly strode from the room.

His lordship ran to the door, but with his hand upon the knob he changed his mind about opening it, for he heard Clovelly humming as he descended the stairs.

CHAPTER IV

THE HORSE THAT
THOUGHT LIKE A MAN

THE CARTER SHOUTED to his team, and it stopped as readily as all horses do when they are pulling a heavy load. The great wheels of the cart lurched back half a yard, struck a stone, and were still.

"Well, sir! Well, sir!" shouted the carter. "Is this a place to stop a cart, on the middle of a hill?"

"I thought that they needed breathing," said Clovelly, and he hastened to add, as the face of the other blackened, "and besides, I want to strike a bargain with you."

"Ah, a bargain? Well, well!"

And he sat with lighted eyes, waiting.

"This nag on the wheel," said Clovelly, "is a stout brute."

He slapped the huge black horse upon the hip and it shrugged its thick hide as if a fly had bitten it.

"He's stout. I warrant you that," the carter declared. "You want to buy him?"

"Just that."

"And what might *you* be needing with a horse like him?"

"I have an uncle," Clovelly explained, smoothly, "who lost his best mare last month, and he's been breaking his heart to find her like ever since. When she leaned against the harness, the plough must come. If it lodged in a root, either the plough cut the root or old Nancy broke the harness. Something had to give when she dug her toes in and squatted her hindquarters. It did a man's heart good to see her work."

21

"I know that kind," said the carter, beaming. "God bless 'em, I know that kind. And here's my Peter, horse, one of the same manners."

"He has the body of Nancy, and even more."

"He's never failed me. But there's no talking, man; I'll never sell Peter. I'd rather sell my wife!"

"Come, come," said Clovelly, and drew out his purse. "Money can persuade a man to most things."

"Not out of his house or his church," asserted the carter, sticking out his jaw, "and not me out of Peter. I know him, and he knows me. I can sleep on the seat all the way home, and Peter will take me to the gate and push the gate open with his nose and go on to the door of the stable. Eh, you scoundrel?"

He prodded Peter with the butt of his whip and Peter cocked a lazy ear by way of answer.

"Well," Clovelly grumbled, "that may be all very true, and I suppose that my uncle must find his own horse."

"Where away does he live?"

"By Old Tew."

"There's heavy land that ways."

"Very heavy. The horses shake their heads at work in those fields and up those hills."

"They do—they do! Well, man, I wish your uncle good fortune."

"But this," said Peter, stepping back and pointing to the lead horse of the tandem, "seems a queer mate to work with an old Trojan like Peter!"

The carter swore a great oath.

"White Harry? Be damned to him! Look at him now, dancing and foaming and fretting. There's no sense to that horse."

"A pretty horse, though," said Clovelly.

It was a great gray stallion, so light in the body color as to deserve the name of "white," but finished with black points all round—every leg being stockinged to knee or hock with black—the muzzle was black also. But the mane and tail were the purest silver.

He stood hardly an inch under seventeen hands, being the full height of the great cart-horse which labored behind him, but his long legs, tapering to slenderness, made him seem much loftier, and he bore his head so high and with such a fiery eye that he appeared all the taller for it.

"He makes a show—he makes a show!" snorted the carter. "But there's no work in him. If he goes down the road, he's lurching first one-side and then the other side to get at a tuft of grass he sees. And if I straighten him out with the whip, he goes rank mad. I've had him smash that harness a good six times, the devil take him!"

The harness, in fact, was a bundle of mendings.

"Too bad!" Clovelly remarked. "Yet he looks like a horse that would pull up a hill."

"Up a hill? There's no holding of him. He tugs the cart onto the heels of Peter. As long as there's a weight behind him, he wants to have the day's work done in a half hour and then be frolicking in the fields. But I'll tell you what's wrong with him, sir. There was never a strap on him 'til he turned six years—that was one year back to this day."

"That's why he filled out like a Hercules," said Clovelly, more to himself than to the carter. "How did it come that he was not used younger—though riding them younger is what thins them out."

"The squire put a saddle on him when he was four. He went mad, threw two men that tried to ride him, and broke the leg of the squire's son. So he was let run in the fields till a year back. Then they tried him again. It was the same thing. He turned into a mad horse. Whips and clubs meant nothing to him. So the squire sold him to me for a song, and I'd sell him willing and quick for a song again."

Clovelly stepped to the head of the lead horse, and White Harry snapped like a tiger at him.

"A high temper," Clovelly observed quietly, "makes a long traveler. I'll give you five pounds for that horse, my friend."

"Five pounds? Five pounds?" cried the carter.

Then he sprang from the seat, ripped the harness from the back of White Harry, and handed the halter to Clovelly.

"I've warned you as I would of warned my brother," he said. "But every man to his fancy. Here's the horse.

"I hope you're one of your word!" he added, balling his fist.

Clovelly placed the money in his hand.

Then he turned up the street without more ado, and brought White Harry into the livery yard which he had located before. There he was fitted with a saddle and a bridle, but Clovelly made them do the work in a stall where the horse had a manger of hay before him, and Clovelly sat in that manger, talking slowly and softly to the stallion all the while.

He held out a handful of oat-heads at last, but what the stallion closed his teeth upon it was upon the arm of the man and not the grain. That great vice pressed for an instant; another bit of effort and the bones of the forearm would have given way. But Clovelly endured without a whisper of complaint.

Then the teeth relaxed their hold and White Harry started back, throwing his head high as if in expectation of a blow, thrusting out a long, stiff upper lip in his fear.

Clovelly, however, did not even look down to his hand. It was paralyzed and would be useless for an hour, or near it. But in the meantime, Clovelly held out more oat-heads in his other hand.

"I see it all," he was saying calmly. "They could not understand the difference. But I do, my lad. There are men of pride and horses of pride. What were whips and clubs and spurs to White Harry, eh? What were curses to him? He could have understood plain talk of a man to a horse well enough? Here, boy, we begin to know each other."

With this, he held forth the oats with a perfect confidence, and behold! White Harry ate them daintily, timidly from his palm—and then ate more—and finally stretched forth his magnificent head with the eyes beginning to grow soft and curious as the eyes of a deer. He sniffed at the hand, at the clothes of Clovelly—and then he looked higher. He sniffed at the man's face. He nibbled at the sable hair.

"Tush, tush!" said Clovelly. "What a rascal you are, White Harry!"

Thereat, he got down from the manger and slapped fierce White Harry upon the breast. No horse likes to be touched there. And Harry, snorting, swung his head around. But instead of snapping with those powerful teeth, he placed his nose against the breast of his new master and sent him staggering back against the wall.

"Hello—hello!" shouted the man with the saddle, who had just come in. "That's a vicious horse, sir. That's a horse I'd watch like a tiger."

"Closer—much closer than any tiger," said Clovelly. "He needs to be watched like a man."

The other gave him a hard look. From his clothes, Clovelly was not more than a poor retainer of a poor family, but from his manner he was much more and from this speech the fellow judged that he might even be a nobleman playing knight errant in disguise. For the gentry were apt to coin just such odd, riddling speeches which appeared to have a meaning and yet had none at all!

Now the saddle was on White Harry. Now Clovelly bridled him. It took a whole hour for those two tasks. But while White Harry pranced and turned and snorted, the man never raised his voice above a low, reassuring tone, and at length White Harry, accoutered for the road, was led forth into the yard. There were twenty persons to watch.

"He'll tear a hole in the sky," one said to another, "when that fellow gets into the saddle."

They had to wait long for that mounting, however, for Clovelly took a half hour of talk and persuasion before at length Harry stood still and permitted the foot of the master to rest in the stirrup. Then Clovelly raised himself gently—and softly, softly he lowered his weight into the saddle and put his foot into the other stirrup.

"Here, sir!" cried the ostler. "You must have a whip, even if you're wild enough to ride without spurs—"

"Get back!" said Clovelly. "If you show this horse a whip, you rascal, I'll use it on your hide so that you'll burn for a fortnight!"

In the meantime, White Harry was trembling in every limb, but he had not quite made up his mind to "tear a hole in the sky." He was entirely willing to do so, but first he waited for the signal of the cut of leather or the torture of spurs.

He waited for yelling, rough voices, and heavy curses. These did not come, either singly or together.

So he turned his head and sniffed at the knee of the new master. Then, in answer to a cautious pull on the rein, he straightened and trotted meekly out of the yard.

CHAPTER V

STAND AND DELIVER

IT HAD BEEN a charming drive, for the roads were firm and not too deeply rutted, and the six well-matched and powerful horses of the baronet dragged his coach along at a round rate. The air was neither cool nor hot; the dust was not thick; and the spirits of the entire party were at the top.

Only Lady Redbourne had—from time to time when the moon sailed behind clouds and the road dipped into some dark hollow, blackened with trees on either side,—leaned over the edge of the carriage and peered anxiously before her and behind to make out intruders along the way. She could see nothing to rest her suspicions upon, but she would not be at ease although her husband laughed roundly at her.

"But, oh," she answered his remonstrances, "one never can tell. They come in bands, Christopher!"

"Well," said Sir Christopher, "if they come in bands large enough to handle my boys—I can only say that they're welcome to what they may take. They'll have earned it—they'll have earned it!"

He indicated the guard which had closed around his coach. There were three tall fellows who rode in front. There were four more, riding two on either side of the coach.

And each of these was heavily armed with pistols and with short-barreled, bell-mouthed carbines which cast a big handful of shot at every charge. They were useless enough at a long range, but in a close encounter those weapons hurled a spray of lead heavy and thick enough to bring down horses and men at once.

Nor were their carbines and their huge horse pistols enough; they were armed, in addition, with long, straight-bladed, basket-hilted broadswords so heavy that, in a dexterous hand, their edge made nothing of a thick helmet.

Besides this vigilant squadron of guards, the two men who sat upon the high driver's seat were equipped with big blun-derbusses and with knives for a close encounter.

The entourage not only made for safety, but with the gay red feathers which flew from their hats and with their flying cloaks and gallant horsemanship they added infinitely to the rich and festive appearance of the equipage. Good Sir Christopher would as soon have traveled without his hat as without his men at arms.

"Do you think, wife," Sir Christopher added, "that a band of cutthroats would stand the close charge of seven such fellows as those?"

"Sixteen of 'em," said his wife, "stopped the king's men who were bringing the tax money in from Bristol last month."

"The king is served by many rascals these days, I fear," Sir Christopher declared. "When those highwaymen showed their faces, the rascals in charge of the money turned their backs and ran like frightened sheep."

"But these men of mine, Herbert," and here he turned to a handsome youth who was with them in the carriage, "these men of mine served through the war. They're old blades and cool heads. They know how to stand a charge and how to push one roundly home. Not a one of them but has carved the Roundheads; not a one of them but has followed Prince Rupert."

Lord Pennistone nodded; he appeared, in fact, more inter-ested in the scenery through which they passed, and gave only a polite attention to the words of his companions.

At length the coach rolled to the gate of the estate. The son of the porter had been waiting to spy them on the road, so that there might be no delay, and as the carriage approached his shout warned his father, and they came up to find the gates already swinging wide.

Through the entrance they rolled, and before them the seven men-at-arms rode like demons, crashing up the driveway.

"Away, boys!" shouted the baronet, waving after them and laughing.

"For," he explained to his lordship, "it's a custom a century old. When we reach the gate, the good fellows who have guarded us race for the house, and the first one to reach the stables gets a double measure of October ale."

"Ah," sighed Lady Redbourne, as they passed smoothly up the avenue among clustering trees, and the heavy gates clanged in the distance behind them, "I cannot help being happier now that we're home. This traveling by night is not at all to my taste."

She added, suddenly: "And what's that? Heavens, Christopher, have we a ghost on the place?"

For here a great white horse drifted among the trunks of the trees just before them and came out onto the road with a shadowy horseman in the saddle.

"It's that rascal Jeremy riding the new gray mare," said Sir Christopher angrily. "He's in love with the creature and cannot keep out of the saddle on her. I'll give him a lesson before we reach the house. By the Lord, he has the effrontery to ride straight towards us! Stop the horses, Clapham!"

The coachman brought the horses to a stop with a shout. He took the clue from the last words of the master and called: "Hello, Jeremy; you're wanted here. Pull up, Jeremy!"

"I'll handle him!" Sir Christopher asserted, standing up in the coach. "Confound the rascal, I'll teach him his duty! He presumes too much. That's the trouble with old servants, Herbert; they become too sure of themselves and their places. And yet," he added, "the mare looks two inches bigger and ten times handsomer than ever. More crest too, eh, Martha?"

His wife had no chance to answer, for the horseman on the

pale gray had obediently drawn rein and came up to them at a slow trot. As he came nearer, he tugged at his hat and a black shadow dropped across his face. At the same time he brought his mount to a full stop and swept two gleaming pistols from his bosom.

"Sir Christopher," he said, "and you two fellows on the driver's seat, the first man of you who moves will be carrying lead with him straightway. Mind you—look sharp, for I have restless fingers upon the triggers of these guns. Ah?"

As he cried out softly with this last word, he fired from his right hand, and with a groan the coachman tumbled from his seat and fell upon the driveway, the blunderbuss which he had attempted to raise and fire being thrown into the brush as he pitched forward.

There was a gasp from Lady Redbourne and exclamations from the men, who arose to leap to the assistance of the fallen man. But the voice of the bandit, speaking as calmly and as steadily as before, controlled them. He had put up the discharged pistol the instant its barrel was empty and snatched another from the holsters on the saddle.

"Stand fast!" he warned them. "Make no quick movements. I detest haste at such a time as this. So put your hands over your heads at once!"

They obeyed, reluctantly.

"Clapham, my poor fellow!" cried Sir Christopher. "Are you murdered?"

"He has only a scratch," said the highwayman. "He is shot through the right thigh with a small bullet which probably did not strike the bone. I am sorry for Clapham, but he acted very bravely and very hastily."

"You, my man—" and he gestured to the footman on the box where Clapham had lately been sitting—"get down and bind up his wound. Mind you, I have my eye upon you constantly. The rest of you step out of the coach one by one. Move slowly, but move steadily."

"Good God," groaned Sir Christopher, "that such a thing should take place upon my own grounds! But my men will be back here at the full speed of their horses; they have heard the explosion of that pistol."

"You are wrong," said the bandit. "The wind was blowing from them to us. Besides, the roaring of their galloping hoofs would almost drown the noise. No, I shall be undisturbed at my work, I hope. Step down, sirs!"

Neither of them moved, as if they debated whether it were not better to attack this strange robber and die fighting than admit on the following day that one man had attacked four armed and vigorous fighters and bested them all. But yonder was the footman kneeling beside Clapham and working over him busily, and now Lady Redbourne set the example by stepping down from the coach and facing the robber.

"We are in the knave's hands, Christopher," she told her husband. "In God's name do nothing rash. We may lose a little money; but money cannot buy back our lost lives. Here are my rings, fellow!"

She stripped them from her fingers and handed them to the masked man.

"You are kind, madame," said he, as her husband and Lord Herbert joined her on the ground. "You are kind, but not quite honest. When you first saw my guns, I observed you make a cherishing gesture toward your throat. Unless I am greatly mistaken, there is something of price clasped upon your bosom, madame."

"You damned rascal!" cried the baronet; "If you touch her, I'll wring your neck for you if it costs me my life."

"Do you argue with me?" the outlaw inquired sternly. "You dare to question me and delay me? I tell you Sir Christopher, that I am in a business for which the penalty is death if I am caught. It is as cheap to kill you, in my eyes, as it is to rob you. And by every devil in hell, if you raise your voice to me again, I'll shoot you through the head."

He spoke this with a softness which made the savagery of the words inexpressibly more terrible than a roaring voice could have been.

"Oh, God!" cried Lady Redbourne. "Christopher, in mercy to me, do not stir foot or hand. Let him have it. Oh, my poor Charley!"

And, with a sob, she drew the necklace from her throat. It was a finely woven gold chain and it suspended a great emerald. The robber moved the hand in which he held it until a glint of the moonlight fell upon it. Then he shut his fingers over it.

"I am sorry for your grief, madame," he told her, "but your tears are hardly worth a thousand pounds, and even the worst villain who ever bought stolen goods would not cheat me so much as to give me less than that sum for this jewel."

"Listen to me, my man," said the baronet. "It was a gift sent to us from our dead boy in India. I'll pay you a thousand guineas ransom—"

"The ransom will take care of itself in due time," the robber interrupted. "In the meantime, your purse, sir."

The baronet snatched out his wallet and cast it angrily upon the ground.

"You will hang, you scoundrel," he assured the bandit. "I shall have the pleasure of seeing you quartered for this night's work."

"Pick up the purse," said the other. "In the name of God, man, do I have to teach good manners to the nobility of England?"

The baronet cursed heavily, but the muzzle of the pistol threatened in no uncertain manner; so he stooped and scooped up the purse and presented it into the hand of the robber.

"Now for you," said the latter, stepping to Pennistone.

"My purse, my ring—and my good wishes," his lordship remarked pleasantly. "And I would pay more than this for a lesson in pistol practice from you, my friend."

"Sir," said the robber, "I am a thousand times grieved that I must discommode so pleasant a gentleman, but it seems to me that you have drawn down the sleeve of your coat with a purpose in mind. I believe that there is something upon your left wrist."

"There is," Herbert Theale admitted in a troubled voice, "a small locket containing a picture which is of no worth to the world but of infinite value to me. I am confident that you will not trouble it."

"A picture?" said the robber. "I have known such trinkets bring a price. I must have it, sir; I must have it at once."

"You may have my life far sooner," said Pennistone. "Of that I assure you."

"I give you warning," began the robber—but here Lord Pennistone sprang at his throat.

It was over before the slow-footed baronet could take a step to help his friend. The long barrel of the pistol cracked against Pennistone's head and he sprawled his length upon the ground. The robber stooped and tore the locket from his wrist. Then he pocketed his spoils and stepped back to his horse.

"I shall have you hounded through England by a hundred men, for this," cried the baronet. "And if you have killed Lord Herbert, you shall be burned alive for it—"

"He is only stunned for a moment," said the robber, keeping one gun directed at them while he fitted his foot into the stirrup. "You see?" For his lordship stirred and groaned where he lay. "And now your men come back in the nick of time to hear the cream of your curses."

Hoofbeats were ringing heavily along the road; the seven had apparently guessed at trouble which delayed the coach so long and they came at full speed to make their inquiry.

"So," said the robber, "au revoir!"

He swung into the saddle and the tall, white horse leaped into the shadows among the trees, followed by a bullet from the pistol of the baronet, which he had snatched out and fired in haste. It was answered by the mocking cheer of the robber as he faded into the woodland.

In the meantime the seven outriders were sweeping up in a

streaming body The baronet directed them after the fugitive with a stream of oaths and promises, and they turned hotly into the forest.

They followed him at a wild speed; a hanging bough knocked one of them from his saddle. The others rushed on unheeding his yell of distress and they came upon the border of the estate in time to see a black-cloaked rider send his great horse at a five foot stone wall and clear it flying.

There was not a one among them who could attempt that feat; and by the time they had dismounted and climbed the wall, the fugitive was a dwindling object far out of range with the moonshine glimmering upon his horse.

CHAPTER VI

A WOMAN'S REPUTATION
AT STAKE

IT WAS CLOSE upon the stroke of midnight, and when the servant entered, Lord Teynham fixed a feverish eye upon him.

"There is some one at the door asking for me," he told his man. "Describe him; give me his features—and tell me first that it is not Milverton."

"It is not."

"For that, the great God be praised. It is a slenderly made, dark-faced man?"

"It is."

"Bring him to me at once—at once."

The servant departed in haste, and his lordship flung himself into a chair and covered his face in his trembling fingers.

"Yet," he groaned, "if he had failed, would he have come to me? Would he not have pocketed the money and disappeared if he had been a rascal—but perhaps he has come to say that he tried, did his best, and could not do enough."

Here the door opened and one in a high-collared cloak and a wide-brimmed hat without a feather entered. He turned down the collar of his cloak at once, and it was the face of Clovelly.

"Quick!" breathed Teynham. "Your luck, man?"

"Lord Pennistone is a gallant fellow," said Clovelly.

"Damn Pennistone!"

"He is worth something more than damning, however."

"The picture! The picture, man!"

"It is here!"

Lord Teynham tore open the face of the locket, stared at the face within it, and then sank into his chair with a gasp of relief. He started erect again, turned the locket to the other side, studied an inscription upon it, and shouted softly in his triumph.

"You are a jewel past the highest price," he told Clovelly. "What did you comb for yourself out of the trick?"

"Some cash," said Clovelly without emotion, "and mighty little credit."

"How was it done?"

"With one bullet."

The face of Teynham blanched, but then he shrugged his shoulders and shook his head.

"Well," he said, "was it Pennistone?"

"Only the coachman; and he will live, if that is what is troubling you."

He seemed to wait with a peculiar anxiety for the answer of Teynham.

"Troubling me? Tush, man; what would the lives of a thousand coachmen be to me?"

There was another tap at the door, which was then opened and the servant announced that Mr. Milverton waited upon his lordship.

"Let him come up. In the meantime, you must not be seen, Clovelly. There is a closet here. I'll leave the door ajar so that you may have air enough."

"I must not stay. If I am followed closely, they'll trap me here."

"There's no other course. Milverton must not see you—must suspect nothing—and Milverton is a fox."

He bustled Clovelly into the closet and had barely secured him there when the door was opened for Milverton. Clovelly watched through the crack in the closet door. He saw a man of the late thirties, rather heavy in body, and with a face whose features were blurred and rendered disagreeable by constant drinking.

It had swollen and flushed his cheeks; it puffed his eyes; it hung a fold of flesh beneath his chin; yet though he was masked with this disagreeable corpulence there was something more attractive about him to the judgment of Clovelly than the regular and perfect features of Lord Teynham. There was still a brightness in his eyes which meant intelligence as well as recklessness, and there was an upright and bold manliness in his bearing.

Such was the appearance of the visitor who entered the apartment of Lord Teynham. He wore a great white peruke, after the new fashion which had been brought in from France and his clothes showed the expenditure of vast time and still vaster money. He cast down in a chair a heavy bag which gave forth a melody of clinking metal as it fell.

"Well, Teynham," he said; "here am I, and here is my money which I agreed to on this damnable bet. I hope to God that you have not breathed a word of it to any one?"

"Not to a soul," said the other. "But why is the bet so damnable? Rochester only last week made a similar one and won it."

"Rochester had to do with a girl of no virtue; we have to do with a saint, my friend."

"You will still maintain her to be so?"

"With my last breath. You do not seriously mean that you have proofs to show me?"

"Milverton, I have!"

The latter lost color.

"Remember," he said sternly, "that to win this bet though you may have manufactured evidence, I shall sift that evidence to the bottom before I believe you. I must do so in self defense. A thousand pounds is not a sum which I can afford to throw away on a whim, but I swear to you, Teynham, that I had rather spend twice that sum than believe a word that might be said against the chastity of sweet Cecily Medhurst!"

"It shows you have a kind heart and a trusting mind, Milverton."

"Don't sneer, Teynham. Damn it, don't sneer. I am touchy to-night. Rochester almost robbed me of my patrimony at dice; and I was about to pay when I bethought me to look at the dice he was using. I had him roll once more and scooped up his cast. They were plainly cogged."

"The devil, Milverton! This will ruin him."

"I thought so, too, for the moment. And during a breathing space, I think the rascal was in doubt as to what he could do to extricate himself. But a lie is never wanting to his tongue. He turned the matter into a laugh with the best grace in the world, assured me that he had not intended to collect the sum he had won from me, and finally I left him."

"So easily?"

"What was there to do? It meant pushing matters to an extreme, otherwise. It was either to let him laugh or else take him out and kill him or be killed by him. I chose not to do that. I hate these damned brawls, Teynham, though I'll fight soon enough to keep my honor whole, I hope.

"Well, here I am, out of temper with the whole realm of England and half inclined to think that every one's a rascal, including myself. But about this wager—I hope you will tell me that the matter is ended here, Teynham. I do assure you that rather than push the affair on, I'll drop all claims to the bet. I was drinking too hard when I made it or such a word could never have passed my lips about Cecily Medhurst!"

"You begin to fear me, I see," sneered Teynham. "But, a week ago, you were confident enough that you had my thousand pounds in your pocket."

The other flushed with anger.

"I see," he said slowly; "that there is nothing for it except to carry the matter to the end. I must examine your proofs, then,

Teynham. Let me have them, my lord. You will prove to me that Cecily has been to you what only a man's wife should be!"

"I shall, Milverton."

"It cannot be, my friend. I tell you, I know her well. I have been in love with her for five years and wooed her more hours than I have courage to confess. If she be not all that is holy and true in womanhood, then I am a fool, a blind man."

"If you were a young man," said his lordship, sneering again, "I should not hesitate to show that you are wrong; but being past boyhood, I am sorry to take an ideal away from you. Nevertheless, what do you think of this, sir!"

And he drew from his pocket and flung carelessly across the table the locket which Clovelly had taken from Lord Herbert Pennistone. Milverton opened the locket and cried out.

"It is her picture, indeed. I remember the very season when it was painted. And yet, my lord, though you may have prevailed upon her to give you such a rare gift, what more does it show?"

"I am a married man, Milverton. Are such gifts made by girls to married men—even though my wife chooses to live in Rome while I stay in London?"

"You shake me," groaned Milverton. "But still I say that this is not quite proof enough."

"Then," said his lordship, "look on the other side."

Milverton turned the locket and read:

"To my dearest, from Cecily."

Then he closed the locket and put it from him with a blank face of suffering.

"I would pay ten years of my life," he said at last; "to be able to forget what I have just now learned."

CHAPTER VII

NOT IN THE BARGAIN

THERE WAS AN interval of pause with no sound except the dry fluttering of a piece of paper which had somewhere been caught in a draft. And it seemed to Clovelly that the reputation of Cecily Medhurst had suddenly become as light and as worthless as that paper.

"And yet," said Milverton, "should she not be punished for this?"

"She has cost you a thousand pounds, I presume?" his lordship remarked carefully.

"Oh, there's the money—there's the money!" exclaimed Milverton. "It's not that—though it hits me hard enough. But to think that while she posed before me as an angel who owned all the virtues as surely as she had the graces at her beck—that such a chit should have blinded me and made me play the fool—and a mere child as she is—why, damn it, Teynham, the longer I think on it the angrier I grow.

"I shall go down to the Swan and Grayhound this night. Some of the lads are gaming and drinking there. I'll let a whisper or two fall; and to-morrow to Man's to buzz again, and before nightfall, if fair Cecily is not carrying her full load of scandal, by the heavens it must be through no fault of mine!"

He stood up.

"You will have some sword drawing in the next fortnight," said Teynham.

"As for that, I should welcome the devil, if he came breathing fire this minute. Cecily false! Cecily abandoned to lies and deceits—her lovely face a mere mask to hide vices as black as those of any of her sex—oh, God, Teynham, I almost wish that I had never made inquiry—that I had kept to my old ignorance. For now I shall be miserable—"

"For a fortnight, or four days, perhaps," suggested his lordship.

The other hesitated.

"Yes," he said finally, "since she is worthless, why should I give her more than enough thought to sink her as low in the eyes of every man as she is now sunk in mine? Yet it is a pity, Teynham—now that our English girls draw infection from the most damned example of those about the king, Louise and Barbara and Nell and the rest, seeing them honored more than queens would be, courted by courtiers and by foreign ambassadors, showered with presents, and hated only by the mob in the dirty streets.

"I say poor England has been so infected that, upon my honor, virtue among its women shrinks every day smaller, and I looked upon Cecily as a breath of sweetness off a meadow of flowers—the last flowers of the summer, mark you. But, God knows, her fall is the more terrible because there was so much farther for her to go! To have been lost in some true love affair that had miscarried—that I could have understood—but to have sinned with you, Teynham, whom all England knows to be already married—oh, it makes the whole picture too horrible. I'm off to the Swan."

"You'll have young Pennistone at you if you open your lips. Better hold the peace, Milverton."

"Odds fish, man, if there were not a fight or two in this, I should be a broken-hearted man in truth. Some good must come out of every fall of fruit."

With this, he waved good night to his host, and stepped from the room, and it seemed to Clovelly that Cecily Medhurst, wherever she lay asleep, must have turned in her bed with a groan of foreboding because a stroke was about to fall upon her worse than death, by far.

He stepped from the closet, and young Lord Teynham swung suddenly about on him, looking up with startled eyes while he clutched at the bag of gold which Milverton had left behind him, It was as if he had forgotten that his assistant in this matter had been hidden in the room throughout the interview.

"Well," he said gruffly, "you see for what stakes I have been playing. And I suppose, Clovelly, that you wish a share of the spoils. But let me assure you that I have a use for every penny of the money. In fact, it came barely in the nick of time, when my creditors were closing in upon me like ravening lions. However, I shall not forget you. You are not hearing the last from me, I promise you."

"As for the money," Clovelly remarked, "I have made enough out of this affair. I have taken an emerald worth five hundred pounds to a rascal who receives stolen goods, and worth a thousand and more from any other rascal in the world. I have two fat purses jammed to the teeth with gold; I have rings in which the jewels alone are worth some hundreds of pounds.

"On the whole, I might look upon the thousand pounds, there, as only your fair share for having directed me to a mine of gold—your share for telling me where to hunt."

"A thousand pounds in one jewel!" cried his lordship with wide eyes. "I may consider my debt to you canceled, then."

"And my debt to you, my lord, is canceled in this."

He counted out forty gold coins and laid the heavy handful upon the table.

"What is the meaning, Clovelly?"

"A simple meaning, which is, of course, that you intend all of this as a jest—you would not blacken the good name of the lady through a trick. You are determined that Milverton shall not speak a whisper against her at the Swan and Greyhound.

"And, therefore, you are sending back to him the money which he has just paid to you on the bet. You are returning his

money, and at the same time, since I have given back your forty pounds, you are giving me, again, the locket which I brought to you."

With this, he laid his hand upon the heavy bag which Milverton had brought and dragged it off the table.

"A thousand devils!" cried the other. "Do you think that I am a fool, Clovelly, to let you walk off with my money as well as your loot?"

"The loot goes back to the place from which it came."

"Shall I take your word for it? Shall I be such an ass as to take your word, Clovelly? Come, come—give me warrant for better sense. Shall I see your threadbare coat and believe in such honesty?"

"As you please."

"If you leave the room with that money, I have only to pull the cord, yonder, to bring a man—"

"One man?"

"And he shall fetch others."

"You will not stir, Teynham. If this is pressed home and I am taken, I have only to tell my story of what you have done; and while I hang for highway robbery, you are worse than hung by the wits and shamed for three generations as a knave and a coward."

The steady insults brought his lordship to his feet, grasping at his sword, but he changed his mind again at once. What he was seeing was that slender ray of light in the hand of this swordsman piercing the aperture of the china plate.

"You will come to wish that you had burned this day in hell," he promised Clovelly, "rather than to have crossed me."

"It may be. A man must take his chances. But in the meantime, you know that I am armed, that I am desperate, that I have gone too far to draw back now, and that one hanging is all they can give for a hundred robberies—or a hundred murders."

He paused, then: "Give me the locket, sir!"

Lord Teynham did not hesitate. He slid the picture across the table, and Clovelly glanced down for the first time into a lovely face with golden hair flowing, and with rich blue eyes. Her smile was so real that it seemed not a picture, but the truth seen at a distance so that the face was small. He dropped the locket into his pocket.

"Good night, Lord Teynham," he said, evenly. "May your spirits be higher when we meet again!"

There was a sound from Teynham as though his rage choked him. Then Clovelly went down the stairs, hearing a bell jingling, at that instant, in the distance. Once it rang and twice and a third time. Instantly doors began to be opened—heavy feet began to run.

Clovelly himself glided hurriedly down the stairs to the lower hall, but the house seemed full of men. One of them was sliding home the great bolt which fastened the front door of the house. Another was running at that instant into the hall from an adjacent room.

And now the voice of Teynham was heard above: "Bring him to me, lads. Bring him living if you can, but if he makes too much noise, bring him in silence—a silent man, my lads! Have no fear. I'll take care of you and answer for what you do in my service. Stop him on the way to the front door—"

There was a chorus of answering voices; a half dozen began to run down the upper hall, while the fellows below, facing around from the door, appeared to spy the shadowy form of Clovelly upon the dim stairs at the same instant and they drew swords.

Clovelly did not hesitate, for if he did not wipe out the obstacle below the millstone from above would catch him and crush him. In his hand there was an impromptu weapon. He swung the heavy bag of gold underhanded, not a hard swing, but an accurate one, for if his aim were true, the weight of the gold would do the rest.

And his aim was true. The bag struck one of the guards full in the breast and skidded him across the floor as if it were greased. He struck the wall with a crash, pitched onto his face, and did not stir.

Then Clovelly came down the stairs like a hawk swooping at his prey. His small sword was out as he ran, and he held it straight before him, as though he intended to split the man before him upon the point. The latter was no craven. He stood his ground manfully, with the immense length of his cut-and-thrust rapier extended straight before him.

No downright charge against such an adversary was in the mind of Clovelly, however. He stopped when he was almost within engaging distance, swerved to the side as the cut of the other swished past his ear, and ran his man fairly through the right shoulder.

The fellow went down in a heap, with a scream of pain, and Clovelly merely paused to scoop up the fallen gold-bag; then he shot back the heavy bolt of the door and stepped into the street, dodging back to avoid falling under the wheels of a passing cart.

CHAPTER VIII

A PARRIED BLOW

"A GIFT FROM heaven," cried Clovelly, and tossing the gold before him, he leaped into the rear of the cart, snatched the reins from the carter, and called to him to lay on the whip.

"And what by all that's sacred might you be, sir?" the carter exclaimed.

Here the door behind them opened, and a half dozen men, muttering like angered bees, spilled out into the street. There was enough starlight filtering down to glint here and there on the steel of their naked weapons.

"A man in fear of his life," Clovelly explained himself, "and if they catch me they'll do for you as well to leave no talkers behind them—"

The carter waited to hear no more, but with a groan of terror he laid on his lash and the clumsy vehicle rocked along its way. But the steed which drew it was hardly more agile or swift of foot than a steer and although it had broken into a lumbering gallop under the lash, it had not yet worked up speed and the pursuers were closing fast, running in a deadly silence.

"No pistols!" gasped one who appeared to be directing the work, "The damned watch might hear. But get him and cut his throat—"

Two who had outsprinted the rest closed rapidly upon the cart and in another instant they would have gained it had not Clovelly, like a keen-eyed charioteer, chosen that instant to swerve the cart into a pitch-black alley, barely wide enough to admit the cart; and the head of the pursuit, following hard, went instantly floundering in the kennels.

They came to the other side with a storm of curses, but the cart and all it contained was now beyond their reach. The honest horse was sweeping along at a speed great enough to defy them, and Clovelly, when he had turned two or three more corners, pressed a coin into the hand of the carter and sprang to the ground with his burden of gold.

He left that good man speechless and gaping after him through the dark, while he made his way straight on for the Swan and the Greyhound. But when he entered, there was no sign of Milverton in the taproom. He inquired for him and was told that he sat upstairs with private company.

"I must see him," said Clovelly.

"What name," the landlord inquired, staring with concern from the head of the newcomer to his feet; "what name, sir, shall I give him?"

"Tell him that a locket and a bag of gold wait for him," said Clovelly, "and I must have an interview with him at once."

The landlord gaped at the bag which Clovelly held, and then managed to laugh as if he understood that it must be only a jest.

"I dare not break in on them unless I am called," he explained to Clovelly.

"Here is courage for you," said Clovelly, and gave him a florin. And so, shaking his head, but working his hand upon the piece of silver as though to actually gain strength of purpose from it, mine host went up the stairs and timidly pushed the door ajar.

Inside, there was a blue swirl of smoke, the sheen of glasses, and the sound of a voice. Mine host drew back a little, shaking his head, but as he turned he found Clovelly had followed and was now beside him.

"Well? Well?" queried the caller.

"I cannot go in," said the landlord. "There's Mr. Milverton making a toast now and he would have my head if I broke in on the middle of his sentence. I know him well, and a great deal of trade he brings to me, and spends his money very freely; but he is hot-tempered, sir."

Indeed, the strong voice of Milverton was clearly audible as he delivered the toast.

"Dear friends," he said, "here is a toast to all light hearts and I thank God for the weights that have been lifted from mine. Here's a toast to one whom I thought was a golden star, but I found her to be a scrap of gilt paper; and I thought her as white as mountain snow, but I find that it is simply an old barn new white-washed.

"I thought there was but one in the world, and that was she, but I find she is one of the thousands. I shall give her name, as one—"

Here there was a scuffle at the door; mine host had clutched in vain, and Clovelly, sliding out of his grip, advanced suddenly into the room.

"And who the devil," exploded Milverton, "are you?"

"One," said Clovelly coolly, "whom you had rather see than the devil, unless devils also can talk to you about lockets and bags of gold."

Milverton uttered an exclamation.

"Friends," he said, "I have news which must be heard. Forgive me. In place of the old toast, here's a new one: To the devil, and may it be long before he finds truer servants!"

It was drunk with a round of laughter in the midst of which Milverton stepped to the side of Clovelly and hurried him into a smaller adjoining room where their privacy was assured by the very volume of the voices which rolled so heavily into the chamber.

"Now, my man," said Milverton, taking his cue from the threadbare clothes of the other, "what under heaven did you mean by that phrase? You come from Lord Teynham, of course."

"I come from him."

"What's your message, then, quickly! I'm burning with a curiosity beyond—"

"The message," said Clovelly, "is chiefly this: His lordship thinks that you will recognize the bag."

He brought it out from beneath his cloak and placed it upon a table. Milverton, with an exclamation, first weighed it in his hand and then untied the mouth of the heavy bag and looked in at the contents as if to make sure that there was no deception.

"If I had been struck dumb, my man," he said to Clovelly, "I could not be more speechless with astonishment. He sends back this money to me?"

"He does, sir."

"With what message, if you please?"

"I believe he presumed that you would understand, sir."

"He sends it to me to speak for itself. This is unlike Teynham. This is not his touch, I should say. But to think of him surrendering a thousand pounds in gold at this time, is like imagining the devil giving up a thousand damned souls secure in his keeping."

"Sir," said Clovelly, "you are doubtless an old friend of his lordship and can interpret his actions better than I. I believe, however, that he intends you to understand the bet which was recently made between you as a jest and not as a serious matter, and that he cannot for a moment keep the thousand pounds. He only retained it so long to give a point to his joke. And I see that I arrived only in time enough to keep that point from having a sting."

Milverton rubbed his knuckles across his forehead.

"I must give up the bottle," he declared, frowning. "My head spins with this news, though I have had hardly a taste after supper. Teynham intended all of this as a jest?"

"He did, sir."

"And where, in the name of heaven, did he get the locket?"

"It was arranged through Lord Pennistone, to whom the locket was given."

"To Pennistone! To Pennistone! Now, God be praised! It clears the poor girl of the stain which I thought rested upon her. And which, had you not arrived when you did—"

He drew a great breath and mopped his forehead again.

"Had you not broken in upon us, I might have done an irreparable harm!"

"So I thought, Mr. Milverton."

"Not that I should have used her name—but I intended to mark her with certain hints which would have started talk buzzing. Because I hate a hypocrite, my man."

"My name," said Clovelly, "is Michael Clovelly."

"I understand you," said Milverton, looking no longer at the threadbare clothes of his companion but squarely into his eyes. "You were named after some Irish relative, and yet I fail to find Ireland in your face."

"Pardon me, I was named after an angel, and yet I suppose that it does not show in my features either."

Milverton laughed.

"Can you tell me how Pennistone was induced to part with this picture that it might be used for a jest? And such a jest!"

"He was induced with a pistol."

"Here is Pelion on Ossa—marvel on marvel! My mild friend Teynham, whose attitude toward guns and swords is so entirely unprofessional, has taken to the road. He has actually braved gallant young Pennistone, whom I know to be a man of men."

"So it seems, sir."

"I still wonder at it. I shall wonder these seven years. It sounds more like a trick of Colonel Blood or one of his ilk."

"There are many on the highways, sir."

"There are, to be sure, but—how was it done?"

"I understand that it was done after the coach of Sir Christopher Redbourne, and his lady and Pennistone with him, had entered his grounds—"

"On his very estate?"

"So I have heard."

"This grows and grows. It will be as big as the ocean in another five minutes. Teynham did such a thing? Never in a thousand years! No, damn me, I know my man. It was not Teynham; it was—why, Clovelly, it was some one with an eye like yours. By Heaven, now, I'll wager you a hundred pounds that you are the man!"

"You honor me," said Clovelly, without changing his expression in the slightest. "However, I shall not claim the honor of shaking hands with Jack Ketch on that account."

"Clovelly, be open to me!"

"In what, Mr. Milverton?"

"It is you who executed this errand. A momentary depression of spirits and purse left you open for an engagement of almost any kind. You fell in with Teynham. He had a desperate need. You played the desperate part. You robbed young Pennistone at the point of a gun; you brought back the loot which was required, and when all was done you suddenly learned the use to which the rascal Teynham was about to put the little painting. Is that not true?"

"I hardly follow your explanation, sir."

"Naturally not," said Milverton dryly. "But when you learned that a lady was to be damned in order that Teynham might have a thousand pounds in his pocket. By the way, how did you get the money away from Teynham?"

"As I said before, Mr. Milverton, Lord Teynham has freely sent me to you with the money in order that no harm may be done to a beautiful and spotless lady."

Milverton paused, then snapped his fingers and shrugged his shoulders.

"Clovelly," he remarked genially, "with every word you speak I become gladder and gladder that I have found you. I shall see you again hereafter. Where are you to be found?"

"Hither and yon," said Clovelly, smiling.

"So? So? Well, then, will you call on me?"

He gave the directions to his lodgings.

"Very gladly."

"Come to-morrow, then. I am waiting on His Grace of Bucks in the late morning. I'll be home again early in the afternoon. Better still, meet me in Paul's Walk. Will you do it?"

"In great hopes, Mr. Milverton."

They saluted each other with a mutual smile, and then Milverton changed his mind again.

"I'll leave this smoky brawl and take a walk with you now in the fresh open. Have you a mind to do that?"

And in five minutes they were on the street together.

CHAPTER IX

DAMNING EVIDENCE

"TELL ME," SAID Milverton, as they stepped into the street, "did you ever see the lovely Cecily in person?"

"Never."

"I guessed it! You judged her only from the miniature, and even from that you knew that she was pure and true."

"I thought I was sure of that."

"How much surer should I have been, my friend, who have known her these years so intimately! And yet when I saw that damnable writing on the back of the locket, and saw that the locket was in the possession of Teynham, I did not doubt any longer. I scorn myself for it!"

They talked of other things. Milverton would gladly have learned something of his companion, but Clovelly would only answer in vague terms. Yet he was free enough to tell of places and countries where he had been; and he seemed to have been everywhere.

He knew even the far land of Mexico on the one hand, and the still more distant realm of India upon the other; and he had seen the curved knives of Afghans and the glass axes of Aztecs. Of such things he chattered freely, but as to the part which he himself had played in every scene, he was extremely reticent. He had simply been there—but why he had been there he would not say.

"By the Lord!" cried Mr. Milverton. "I have it at last; you have been a sailor."

"I have been at sea," said Clovelly.

"You are still behind a wall, eh?" murmured Milverton. "Well," he added, "I shall not try to draw you out into the open. As a matter of fact, I have been hoping that there was something in which I could serve you well; but since there seems to be nothing, I must even let you go on your own way."

He was silent for a long moment after this, as though in pique, but suddenly he murmured: "There's the house Medhurst has taken since he came down from the country. Behind that wall is his garden."

"He's rich, then, to have a place of such a size in London."

"He's as rich as the devil himself. He had estates enough before the war, but during the war he was wrecked completely because he clung so steadfastly to the cause of the king and would yield not a step to the powers of the commonwealth. He had to run into Scotland, leaving Cecily behind to take care of herself, poor child, while her father took care of the king.

"Came down to Worcester and he was with the king during part of the flight. As a matter of fact, he let himself be taken, at one point in the flight, to give his majesty time to put a little distance between himself and the Roundheads. He was thrown in prison and then ordered beheaded as a traitor; but he escaped, fled overseas, and joined King Charles on the Continent.

"Since the restoration of the old line of kings, you know that Old Rowley can easily forget the cavaliers who fought for his father and even the best of those who fought for himself, but he cannot forget those who gave him personal services. So Medhurst could have had what he wanted. Old Rowley would have made him a lord if he had said the word, but Medhurst is prouder of being a Medhurst than he would be of being the Duke of York. The family goes back, according to him, to the Conquest; he has even traced them into a dimmer past than that.

"So he preferred to remain a mere gentleman, saying that his coat of arms was to him a greater thing than any title. But he admitted that he would be glad enough to enlarge his deer park.

"Old Rowley acted on that hint. All the confiscations of Roundheads in the neighborhood were turned to the advantage of Medhurst. His estate puffed out on all sides. In a fortnight he became a very rich man.

"That was not all. He felt that the true glory of England was on the seas. So he fitted out a big ship at his own expense, sent her to the Spanish Main, and she had not been a week in those waters when she came afoul of a treasure ship loaded to the gunwales with gold and silver bullion. That treasure was brought home to Medhurst Park; and since then old Geoffrey Medhurst has had more than he knows what to do with. So he put a quantity into mercantile adventures, and, by Heaven, whatever he touches is straightway turned into gold! The man has the hand of Midas, in truth. And so, as you can see, he can afford to come to London and rent a house with a garden—aye, half a dozen gardens, if he had a mind to them."

He was rambling on in this fashion about the lucky old cavalier when Clovelly clapped him suddenly upon the shoulder and tugged him flat against the garden wall. Vines rolled over the top and dropped streamers about them, so they were both, in the darkness, very thoroughly obscured. They had hardly stepped there when the quick and startling action of Clovelly was explained to Milverton by the opening of a little gate in the wall not three paces in front of them.

A man stepped out, looked up and down the street, and then twisted his cloak about him.

"God be praised, Cecily!" he said. "There is no one to mark my going. In again and out again without so much as a finger pointed toward me. I am a lucky man!"

"By the gods of damnation!" whispered Milverton.

"What was that?" asked the faint and frightened voice of the girl.

"A breath of wind through the leaves," said the stranger.

"A promise of the deepest pit in hell for you!" gasped Milverton.

But here Clovelly trod heavily upon his foot, and he was silent perforce.

"Come to me again, and come soon, Ned!"

"God help me to come soon—soon, Cecily."

"And with such good news again!"

"Good or bad, I'll bring them."

"I thank you from the bottom of my heart."

"Hush! It is I who thank you for the glimpse of heaven now and again. I shall come at a more seasonable hour the next time, however."

"What are time and the hour to me?" asked Cecily in a sort of transport. "When I see you, I shall forget the season of day and night. Remember!"

"I shall never forget to-night. Farewell a while, Cecily."

"Be it short, Ned."

"It's Marberry!" whispered the furious man at the shoulder of Clovelly. "It's that loose-living fiend—that devilish libertine—Marberry, of all the world!"

"Good night," the stranger softly cried.

"Good night, and God bless you," the girl replied.

The gate closed. Marberry stood for a moment in the shadow of it with his head thrown back and his hands pressed to his heart in exultation. Then he turned and went slowly down the street, just past the hidden two, pausing now and again in his walk and drawing a deep breath as though a thought of inexpressible delight came to him. As he passed, Milverton stirred to go after him, but a hand of iron took his arm and froze him to his place.

Marberry turned the corner and was gone.

"Let me after him!" groaned Milverton. "Oh, damn him, I'll have the innermost blood of his heart for this!"

"Why should you claim it?" asked Clovelly harshly. "I have

a claim myself. We'll throw dice to-night to see which of us shall kill him to-morrow."

"You are right," said the other after a moment of thought. "It is not fair to attack him to-night, when his head is in a whirl with other things. But to-morrow I shall find and kill the rat. Or else the dice give that exquisite privilege to you, Clovelly."

"But, ah—where is our flower of lovely innocence, Clovelly? Where is the lady we both have dreamed a dream about? The lie of Teynham was a true lie after all.

"But with Marberry! To have sinned with him—that common rake and light of love—that damned old wrinkled villain! There is nothing but the blackness of his vices to make him differ from other men; there is nothing but the fame of the number of his loves to have brought him to her attention.

"I tell you, Clovelly, Teynham saw the truth in her, even though he lied about himself. The eye of a lecher will mark down the lecherous, even in a glance. But alas, poor old Medhurst! He will go mad with grief and shame if ever he learns of this."

"Should he know?" asked Clovelly.

"I wonder. What a torture—what a blight upon the happiness of his fortunes!"

"And yet if he does not know, she may be more deeply lost because she is unwatched."

"Lost? How could she be more deeply lost, man? Can you paint a shadow upon black? Is there anything darker than soot? There are no degrees of sin in a woman. When she is once lost, she cannot be more deeply damned. And yet—I think you are right. Poor old Geoffrey! He must know. Here's for him. Yonder is his room just above us."

They had come under the arch of an overhanging window which stood deep upon the street, and Milverton scraped up a handful of pebbles and began to throw them one by one up against the panes. Finally they heard a groan and then an oath from the room above. The floor creaked and finally the window was thrown open.

"What's down there in the street, in the devil's name? Who are you?"

Clovelly made out a great shaggy head, a pair of wide shoulders, a face covered with beard and mustache, either very gray or altogether white, though the voice was as resonant as that of a man not far past middle age.

"Look to your daughter, Medhurst," called Milverton softly.

"What? To Cecily? What of her? And who are you that tell me?"

"Look to the garden. Say one word to her."

"What word? What's this mummery about?"

"Say the word 'Marberry' to her. And then watch her face."

There was an instant's pause, and then in silence the window was closed; they went slowly on together.

CHAPTER X

THE POISON OF THE TIMES

SILENCE AND SOFT ways were not in the ordinary course of the nature of Geoffrey Medhurst. But now when he closed the window without a word it was because a sudden faintness had fallen upon him. He reached a chair and lowered himself into it, his stout arms shaking under the weight of his body; and there he sat for a long moment, trying to think, but not daring to focus his mind. When he arose, it was with a start, as though out of a dream. He threw a thick dressing gown around his shoulders, dropped a small pistol into one of the deep pockets, and, stepping into slippers, he scuffed to the door, opened it, and looked down the hall. There was before him the guilty and secret silence of the night, and all at once all things were possible, even the most damned.

He went straight down the passage to its end and so descended by a curved and narrow flight of steps to the garden door; but before he reached it, it was opened. The moon broke through the cloud at that instant, and it shone dazzling upon the white-clad form of Cecily, and it made silver of her golden hair.

To her father, she looked more like an angel than flesh and blood. He could not move—he could not speak—so terrible was the strife in his soul.

And so she started up the stairs and did not see him until she was almost upon him. She came so near that he breathed the scent of the fresh outdoors upon her, and it seemed to his aching heart that it was sweeter than any perfume of flowers. But now she recoiled with a gasp of fear; and when he heard the sound he was able to speak for the first time.

"Come up to your room," he commanded, and he led the way.

"Is there bad news? Is there bad news?" she was murmuring behind him; but it seemed to Medhurst that there was a strange tremor in her voice.

He went to the door of her chamber, but when his hand was upon the knob he could not enter the room. He had himself prepared it for her coming, for he had gone on ahead to London, taken this house, and furnished it for her. He had gone shopping and bought with his own hands for her.

He had made it a bright room, a light and happy room, and when he thought of taking her into that place now and con- fronting her with the horrible and dark suspicion which the two men upon the street had planted in his mind, his courage failed him.

"Not here," he muttered, and took her into a small sitting room on the opposite side of the hall.

It was nearly as bad, however, for when he had kindled a light he saw that she had appropriated the room to herself with a half dozen little touches. In the shadows of one corner red roses were burning; yonder was a workbasket, and on top of all was a bit of hand-made lace so delicately woven that it seemed that fairy fingers must have woven it.

Upon a table was a bonnet; beside it were plumes of various lengths, varying color; and a pair of small slippers sat demure- ly beside the hearth. Geoffrey Medhurst looked upon all these things and then upon his daughter. And when he saw her, peace flowed in upon his heart; the ache left his throat.

For when loveliness passes a certain point, it begins to be partly holiness. He felt with a great wave of joy that he had not even the right to question her. Indeed, he would gladly have turned the whole thing off, if he could have done so, but, having brought her here in such a solemn manner that her eyes were wide and frightened upon him, he had to find something to say; and as an inventor of lies he had always shown the greatest poverty of mind.

For he was essentially a bluff man. His body was armed with two strong hands to take what he wanted in the world, and his mind was very much the same. It was designed to grasp and to possess with a single gesture; it was not intended for delicate fencing. He could only tell her the truth of his suspicions.

"Cecily," he said, clearing his throat and beginning to wish that the two strangers were in a bottomless pit—"Cecily, this is an odd hour for wandering in the garden, my dear."

"But you know that I love a garden by night even more than by day, sir."

"But the hour, Cecily."

"I haven't the least idea, I'm sure."

"It's a full hour past midnight."

"No, no! So late?"

She made a gesture of wonder and opened her eyes at him, but a smile was just out of sight upon her lips. He felt it coming, and had to set his teeth to keep from smiling himself.

"Yes," he answered her—"very late. You must not go into the garden at such a time, Cecily. You must know that. Even your wild, impracticable brain must know that."

"Why not? The wall is far too high for a thief to get in."

"But the night—it's so damned, ghostly still, Cecily."

She laughed frankly at him.

"Does that make it a sin to be in the garden, sir?"

"Well, well, well!" he said. "After all—"

"You frightened me terribly, standing on the stairs like that without a word," she sighed.

If there was assurance in her manner, there was just a shadow of relief in it, also; and he remembered the last suggestion of the voice from the street.

"There is another thing," he said, and he summoned a frown. A frown on his face was particularly black, for when he lowered his bushy white brows his eyes were turned to shadows with two points of light glittering forth. "There is another thing and that is—'Marberry!'"

He cast into his tone all the sinister meaning which he could summon, but he could not have been prepared for the effect which it produced. Cecily cried out in a small, shrill voice of terror, regarded him as though he were a ghost, and then fled from the room.

He overtook her at her door. He caught her by both wrists, placed them in one of his great hands, and dragged her back to the sitting room, without a word. For he was far past speech. There he flung her into a chair and stood above her.

"Now," he managed to say: "Talk! Talk in the name of God, Cecily. I'm in a mood for killing."

She was twisting her hands together and then tearing them apart.

"I—I—I'm trying to talk, sir."

"A lie, Cecily. Any quick, clever lie to keep me from a murder! Marberry was here."

"Innocently. I swear to God, innocently."

"Innocent? Marberry? When he speaks to a woman it's enough to besmirch her and make her the talk of the town. Marberry here—in the middle of the night! Talk, Cecily! A lie and a good lie, for you're near dying and I'm near hanging! God, God, why was I born?"

"It—was—Oliver Perth—" she managed to gasp.

"Perth? You mean to tell me that Marberry was here on the business of another man?"

"It seems madness—but oh, believe me! In the wars, Oliver did Marberry a great service and Marberry swore to repay him if ever he could. And one way he could do it; that was to bring me a message from poor Oliver. There was no other way to come to me save in the night because Marberry knows that you hate him and would never let him enter the house—"

"Would a man let the plague enter his house? Go on, Cecily. I listen. I pray to believe!"

"So he came to-night and he—he found me in the garden."

"A lucky chance, eh?"

"A—chance. Yes!"

"And what did he say to you—from the damned Roundhead Perth?"

"He said—that—that Oliver was mad with grief because you had taken me away from him to London."

"So?"

"And Oliver wanted to know if I had come of my own free will."

"So you told him—?"

"That it was not of my free will. God knows that that is the truth, sir!"

"Get on with the story. What else?"

"That if it were not of my free will, Oliver would come for me a week from this day, and that I should be willing and ready to go with him."

"You said you would go?"

"I said that I could not go by stealth in the middle of the night. That—that it was like stabbing my dear father when his back was turned."

"No more of that!"

"But that if he came, I should see him."

"And then?"

"And then Mr. Marberry left me."

"You lie, Cecily!"

"On my honor!"

"Cecily," he cried fiercely, "you lie, for I was watching all the time."

He strode to her as he spoke and leaned above her, but, though she trembled, her eyes held steadfastly upon his own.

"I swear that he left me then—by the honor of my mother!"

At this he recoiled from her, crying out beneath his breath.

"You cunning, shameless devil, to conjure me with that thought at such a time. God be praised that poor Sylvia died before this curse descended upon our house."

"Sir, what can I do to make you believe me?"

"Nothing! If a white angel came and stood beside you and repeated your words and swore to them, I'd still know that you lied. For the poison of the times has spread to Medhurst Park and found even my daughter. God teach me what to do—teach me what to do!"

And he threw his long arms above his head, imploring help. When his hands fell to his sides again he appeared calmer.

"You will not confess?"

"There is nothing more to confess. I have told you all the truth—every word, on my soul."

"Go to your room," he said at last. "Go to your room, and if you can remember a prayer, say it for the salvation of your lost life, girl. Pray to God to teach me what to do, as I shall pray."

And so he stalked from the room, and she heard his heavy stride go down the hall, heard his door opened and shut with a jar that sent a shiver through the house. And, now that he was gone, it seemed that strength ran through her body.

She started to her feet and fled down the hall to his door, but with her hand upon it, she hesitated; and as she waited, she felt, rather than heard, a tremor of soft sound beginning— something that shook her to the heart, and then she knew that it was the muffled sobbing of her father.

She turned away, at that, and crept slowly back to her room, and there she sat crouched into a chair, waiting and watching until the furniture in the room began to take a shape in the dimness, ebony shapes, half-blurred. And then she could see the great copper beech tree in the garden.

But the light grew; the leaves of the beech began to send forth a faint, cold luster; far off bells began to chime, made into a soft murmur by the distance, and so at length she knew that the day had come and found her and that she had reached the end of her rest. There was no place to which she could flee.

THE POWER BEHIND
THE THRONE

THE ANTECHAMBERS OFFERED a scene which would have flattered the vanity of a king, even such a king as young Louis who had seized the reigns of power in France and announced that he was the state.

There were jockeys come to sell horses to this English duke, or to announce the price of a charger after which he had made inquiry; there were poets, sitting with an inward eye while they conned again the little ode of lavish praise which they had composed; there were pages sent from great houses, brilliant in livery, bold as sword blades and as keen, wandering here and there with a letter stuck in their caps, which they had been made to vow they would give into no hand saving that of the great man himself.

More this this, there were sage politicians, looking askance at one another as though they would probe the secrets which had called them all hitherto; and there were others stiffened with age, dour of aspect, looking steadfastly down upon the floor, and these were old soldiers who had been forced by the pressure of bitter circumstances to come hither for aid.

Presently a whisper came from an unknown source, and the lively chattering ceased on an instant and each man began to turn hastily in his mind the scheme or the thought which had brought him here. For the soldiers were aware that they were to confront one who had been a warrior not without success; the wits knew that he was a wit far surpassing their own efforts;

the poets knew that his taste could plumb their verses to the bottom and make or break them with an epigram that day, perhaps spoken in the royal presence where all words became weighty; and the statesmen understood that they were about to face one who had shown upon a hundred occasions a temper and a conscience as slippery and as cunning as the famed old serpent's.

The whisper was that his grace was now on the point of waking, and in fact the object of all this concern had even then turned over in his bed, hurled back the curtains, and, lounging upon the pillows, looked lazily and unhappily about the room.

"Randal!" he groaned at last.

"Yes?" said a voice just at his head, and moving his eyes he discovered that his valet had been standing at the very head of the bed waiting like a statue.

"Statues and devils!" muttered the Duke of Ipswich. "How long have you been standing there?"

"Something over an hour, sir."

"Without moving?"

"Without moving."

"It makes my head spin. Why the devil should you do that? Don't your legs give out?"

"I do it, your grace, because if I were a step away—"

"Well, well?"

"The devil would have me, sir."

His grace pressed a hand against his forehead.

"An hour later," he said, "I presume that I shall smile at that remark. In the meantime, Randal, I hate mirth as I hate the fiend before noon."

"It is just verging past noon, sir."

"So late. Damn me, Randal, I must give up these heavy Spanish wines. They send a fog over the brain out of which a man cannot walk for two days."

So saying, he slowly sat up in the bed, propping himself upon rather uncertain arms, and as he gained a vertical position, he groaned and wrinkled his face into an expression of pain.

"A wet cloth for the head, sir?" suggested Randal.

It was, in fact, the very thought which had come into the brain of his grace, but since another suggested it, he shook his head and cursed again when the motion tormented him.

"Wrong, Randal, wrong," he said. "What is a heavy head in the morning to me? Odd's fish, as Old Rowley would say, have I not been a soldier?"

And he began to laugh, carefully, lest the effort should rack his sore head. He now forced himself to stand up, and thrust his arms into the gown which Randal held out to him, pushed his feet into large, furred slippers, and stretched himself slowly, delicately, limb by limb.

He was a man in the early middle of life. He had once been remarkably handsome, and dissipation had not yet completely blurred and extinguished his good looks.

He was still heavily flushed from the last night's carouse, but he forced himself with a tottering step to cross the floor to an adjoining antechamber, where he washed his face and came out again walking straight and light, no matter at what a cost. And Randal wondered at him; until he remembered that those who court a king, and particularly such a capricious monarch as Charles the Second, are forced to forget their own feelings.

Around that luxurious king, every loose-living courtier was forced to consider his own desires last and the merry monarch's first. This training now served his grace in good stead. He wrapped the robe around him, and lounged again on the bed against the pillows which Randal had in the meantime piled for him.

"What letters have come?" he asked languidly.

"These."

Randal presented with all respect a great silver tray upon which letters of every color and texture, and sealed with every manner of seal, were heaped, not by the handful but literally by the score. His grace reached out and knocked half a hundred envelopes upon the coverlet which lay across his knees. From these he picked out two or three.

"Open and read these, Randal; there may be something in them. As for the rest, burn them, and be damned. Women who write letters at night are such fools in the day that I hate to see 'em. What is that?"

Randal began to read:

> "Dear G:
> "I have sudden news that H.M. has heard of your dealings in Portugal and that he is very angry. Avoid him until you have supplied yourself with your best vein of conversation so that when you meet Rowley again you may drown his anger in laughter.
> "In all kindness,
> "R."

"The imp Rochester again!" cried Ipswich. "He is in the business of all men. He can make himself as small as a gnat and creep through the keyholes into the council chambers of the great. He can live in the color which dances in the heart of a glass of wine and so draw forth the inmost secrets of the loose-livers. He has upon his shoulders a cloak of a thousand colors and can change them all at will.

"It is a greater gift than to be able to walk invisible; for it means that wherever he goes he can make himself welcomed. His satire is like the claws of the devil; but since he has chosen to commend himself to me by this service, I shall remember him. Put him down in my book of the saved."

Randal, with all gravity, stepped to a cabinet and drew forth a small volume which he opened.

"Is there mention of him yet?"

"Not a word, my lord."

"But he is entered more than once in my book of the damned. He has lashed me with that tongue of his more than once. But I trust that I have paid all back with him. How shall I mark him down in the book of the saved? With a great cross, Randal, or with a small one?"

"A great cross, my lord, I presume."

"You presume wrong. With a small cross."

"But to warn you that the king—"

"Tush, the king knows already everything that I have done in Portugal. This is merely Rochester's way of telling me that he knows also, and in fact, he could make it damnably awkward for me if he chose so to do. A small cross, Randal."

The valet inscribed the mark under the name of Rochester in due course, and returning to the bedside of his master, he picked up again the letters which he was to read, but his grace had by this time changed his mind.

"The devil fly away with the letters," he said. "When a man has anything worth saying, he is sure to come to speak it in person. Go look without, Randal, and bring in one of those who wait to see me."

"Which one, sir?"

"Are there many?"

"If you listen closely, you cannot fail to hear them stir and murmur, sir."

His grace closed his eyes and listened to the sounds which were felt rather than heard from beyond the wall.

"I am not quite forgotten, it seems," he remarked without smiling, but with an indescribable joy. He continued without opening his eyes: "Bring in the oldest man you see. I am in a grave humor this morning!"

CHAPTER XII

C FOR CECILY!

THE DOOR OPENED, there was a pause, and then a slow and heavy step entered the room. His grace looked up and saw before him an upright veteran who must have been close to his eightieth year.

When he felt the eye of the duke upon him, he bowed low and then straightened solemnly and remained with his heels drawn together like a soldier and his eyes fixed not upon the duke, but upon some object just beneath his face.

"Well?" said his grace. "Well, my friend?"

"You have forgotten me, I see," replied a deep and rolling bass voice.

"Not that voice!" cried Ipswich: "By heaven, something is about to break upon my memory—it is gone! But who are you, then?"

"The fight was close, and you had rolled from your horse; the Roundhead rose above you and aimed his stroke—"

"God of the Spartans!" cried his grace, so far excited that he raised himself upon one elbow. "I recall it all now. Against that blow I was for the moment helpless; and you, since both of your arms were wounded so that they could not be raised, put your head beneath the blow and so saved my life at the horrible risking of your own—I recall it now perfectly well. But, my dear friend, where have you been? Why have I not seen your face?"

So saying, he examined the garments and the condition of the other with a searching eye. The cloth was not rich, but it

71

was soberly stout, and the fashion of the making was good. Certainly he was not in the last grip of poverty, and the duke sighed in spite of himself. He had given away much and lavished still more upon his own pleasures and every extra drain was now a terrible burden.

"And yet," he said kindly, "I have misplaced your name, though it is something upon which I put the highest value. I have misplaced your name, but if you will supply it to me, I shall endeavor to prove to you that I carry the recollection of what you have performed for me close to my heart."

"I am Richard Leighton," said the other.

"Leighton? Ay, that is the name. That is the name. My friend and old companion, I am a thousand times happy in the sight of you. Is it a lucky chance which has brought you to see me or do you, in fact, lie in need of some service which I shall most happily render you?"

The old man flushed heavily and began to speak two or three times before he was successful in making an audible sound.

"I have a son named John, who is better known as Jack Leighton," he said, and paused as if this should convey some intelligence to the ears of his listener.

"Leighton? Jack Leighton?"

"By some he is called Captain Jack," said the old man, almost under his breath.

"All the saints defend him! Not Jack Leighton? Not the highwayman?"

"The same, my lord."

"Now, God pity him and you, too."

"It is not pity—it is mercy that I require."

"When is the unhappy hour?"

"He is to be executed to-morrow."

"You have drawn a fine bow here, friend."

"I have waited until the last moment before I called upon your aid."

"Down, pride, down!" cried his grace. "Consider my hand as your hand and my purse as your purse from this moment. There is no shame between hand and hand, if one help the other, eh? Tush! Have no fear. I shall go to his majesty this very hour and it shall go hard if I cannot win away one life from his justice. What, man, no tears!"

"I cannot help it," said the old fellow in a stifled voice, hanging his head. "When I think of your kindness and of his majesty's blessed mercy—how differing from the hard hearts of those who took one sacred life?"

He raised his tear-stained face as though the picture of the first Charles upon the scaffold had been revealed to him at that moment. His grace, somewhat affected, stretched out his hand to terminate an interview which was beginning to grow painful, and, as he did so, prevented Leighton from kissing the finger of his benefactor. The duke clasped the hand of the old man instead, and beckoned to Randal to lead the veteran from the room by a private door which would enable him to escape the observation of those who still waited without.

"Because," said his grace, when Randal had executed this service and returned, "the tears of such an old hero are sacred things and not to be seen by scum such as those who wait outside. But Captain Jack—what a son from what a father. Well, well!

"I'll read again, and see no more. Bid the crowd go—that I'll not face them today if they stay till the dark."

"Shall I tell them that your grace is ill?"

"Tell them nothing. I am in a peremptory humor and, by God, I shall make me no excuses. Tell them to be off, and no more!"

With this, he scowled at the lofty door which communicated with the anterooms and turned to the letters of the morning again.

"Here," he said, as Randal returned, "is a rascal unknown to me who has the effrontery to write me a letter fat enough to pass as a loaf of bread. Who the devil may this be? Some ranting, canting Roundhead has sent me a reproof from overseas, no doubt!"

He ripped it open, read a few lines, began to laugh, read still more, and then followed it through to the end, after which with a complacent smile, and with a distant and thoughtful eye, he placed the letter in the pocket of his gown.

"Randal!" he called.

"Yes, my lord?"

"Clear away the rest of this junk heap of mail. I have found a letter which is a masterpiece and all else would fall flat after it. I am through with the mail. I must see some one—talk with some one—what the devil, Randal—have you sent them away from the anterooms?"

"You gave me a most particular order, Sir."

"Order? Order? An order is given with the eye and not with the tongue. I did not look at you when I spoke. By heaven, Randal, if you cannot read me better than this, I must put you in charge of a farm for me."

"Your order," said Randal, continuing, "seemed particular, but I bore in mind that your heart might not be in it and therefore I presumed not to tell them to begone."

"You presumed so much? You presume very far, Randal," said the petulant nobleman. "However, since they are still there, I shall see one more. Whom did I see last? Leighton, the oldest man there. I shall see the youngest, now. Bring in the youngest of them all."

Randal accordingly departed, and returned again, ushering in a slender youngster dressed dazzlingly in black and scarlet with a great hat and a scarlet feather upon his head. He swept off his hat and made a low bow.

With the removal of the hat, his face for the first time became really visible, and his grace uttered an exclamation, and waved to Randal, who required no other hint, but turned his back and fled from the room.

"Beatrice," muttered his grace, before Randal was indeed out of earshot. "Beatrice, what wild and fantastic spirit has brought you here?"

As the seeming page loosed the cloak and sat down crossing the slender, scarlet-hosed legs, it was plain that no man since the beginning of time was ever so finely made.

"My dear George," she answered him, joining the tips of her fingers beneath her chin, "it is a matter of no importance. I told Jerry Mallow that I would see you in your bedroom and tell him the pattern of your robe to prove it."

"Child, child!" cried his grace, "you will have yourself talked of in every coffee house—in every tavern."

"Who'll begin it?" she said carelessly.

"Mallow, of course."

"If he dare, you'll kill him, George."

"I can't kill half of London, Beatrice."

She rose and stamped her foot.

"You are stupid this morning, George. Do you think I have come all this way to be criticized?"

"My dear, only a fool could criticize you."

She tossed her pretty head at this and her great, bold eyes twinkled at him.

"That's better, but not very well. Kiss me good-by, George, and I'll be gone again."

She stepped into his arms as she spoke, but Ipswich touched only the gleam of her black hair with his lips.

"If I kissed you now, Beatrice," he told her, "I should have to spend all the rest of the day in the dark of the moon. Let me kiss you to-night, and the whole day shall be a song."

"Oh George," said she, "what a liar you are—what a glorious one, however."

And with this, she was away through the side door of the room, almost as if she had been through it before. Randal returned to find his grace in high ill humor.

"I shall never see her again," he was vowing. "When a young chit takes the first liberty with a man, he might as well cross her off his book. The cost of enduring her tongue from that moment is greater than any joy from looking at her silly face. Write that down, Randal."

"I shall never forget it, sir."

"Was she noticed in the anterooms, Randal?"

"I think not, sir. She was carrying it off with such a pretty dash, strutting up and down and never shrinking in a corner, that I think no one dared to suspect her of being a woman."

"Let me see a man, now, and a man's man, to get the taste of this folly out of my mind!"

"What manner of a man's man, sir?"

"Name some who are waiting?"

"There's Mr. Bishop."

"I hate to listen to these long-winded droners—these explorers by sea. Why should I care if he can sail to China by the northwest passage or by jumping over the moon? The devil take him! Who else?"

"Mr. Milverton."

"He's a fellow too weary with things as he finds them."

"I believe you asked him to call on you this morning."

"I have forgotten for what, and the devil fly away with appointments. Never forget that, Randal. I hold myself superior to appointments with any man in the kingdom saving with Old Rowley himself."

"I shall remember, sir."

"Who else?"

"A tall, dark-faced man."

"His name?"

"He is unknown to me."

"Why do you speak of him, then?"

"When he jostled the wounded arm of Mr. Milverton—"

"Is Milverton's arm wounded?"

"His left arm, sir."

"No matter, then."

"In fact, sir, it was his right."

"His right arm wounded? Have him in. There'll be a story in this."

So Milverton was brought into the room, and waved a cheerful greeting to his lordship. For Milverton was a gay and saucy fellow who appeared to pay no attention to people of rank and of title.

"You were done for—and this morning at sunrise," said his grace.

"Neatly done, too, and by a fellow I counted on killing with ease," said Milverton. "However, I shall learn a trick or two from a new master I have found and then show Marberry what a consummate ass he was not to finish me off. I'll pay him for his great mercy with half a yard of steel through his belly."

His grace laughed without measure at the calloused frankness of this avowal.

"Well, Milverton," he said, "you are a rare one in this little island. You are the only man I know who speaks what he thinks and thinks what he speaks."

"At times, sir."

"Except to the ladies, of course."

"I have told my last lie to a lady!"

"How so, Milverton?"

"They're not worth the trouble of invention, your grace. Better to let them have the facts and let them digest them or not as they please. Am I wrong?"

"Perhaps there is something in that, also. It was because of a woman you fought?"

"It was."

"I would give my best sword blade for her name."

"I cannot give it to you; besides, you have never heard of her."

"Her initials only, then."

"Her first name begins with C. I can tell you no more."

"C for Clarissa; no? For Cecily, then.

"By heavens, Milverton, you start and change color! Cecily her first name, and—Medhurst her last?"

CHAPTER XIII

HER FATHER'S FRIEND

THE AMAZEMENT OF the caller was almost terror, and he stared with great eyes of awe until the duke burst into irrepressible laughter.

"Here are two coincidences," he said, "which have come pat, one upon the other, and yet if I were to use them carefully I could build up a name for myself as a man of omniscient knowledge. Is it not true?"

"It is very true, your grace," said Milverton, still abashed in spite of the merry laughter of Ipswich. "I cannot tell how in the course of all that is wonderful you could have learned the bottom of this affair!"

"I did not—I did not, my friend. I partly guessed and partly jumped at a chance. I remembered having heard you speak of the Medhursts as friends of yours. But let's get back to Marberry. What has become of that rascal? After besting you he got clean away, I have no doubt?"

Milverton smiled with a sour satisfaction.

"I had with me," he said, "a certain second."

"Come, come," murmured his grace, "you speak as if you had carried divine lightning in your bare hand."

"At least," said Milverton, "to Marberry it must have seemed that he was struck down by fires from heaven; from heaven only could such swordsmanship have come!"

The duke raised his head with a new light in his eye. He was himself a swordsman of celebrated and deadly elegance, and had proved his skill as well in foil-play as in mortal encounters.

"Who is this new paragon?" he asked eagerly. "Who was your second, Milverton?""

"A man of whom you have never heard."

"Come, come! I have already guessed one of your secrets. I'll worm out the other in a moment. Tell me his name, Milverton."

"His name, your grace, is Michael Clovelly."

His grace lifted his glance, while he examined his memory swiftly and thoroughly.

"It is the name of some new master," he said slowly, "if indeed he be a master. But in one encounter, how could that be proved?"

"You will consider Marberry a good blade?"

"Well enough," said the duke grudgingly. "But a precisian in the French school. He fights by rule, though with an infinite amount of practice."

"I would grant him even more talents than that," said Milverton with a sigh, "and I believe you would have done so also, had you seen him handle me. I was a child in his hands.

"But when he in turn stepped out against Clovelly, the tale was far different. Clovelly walked up to him as though for a friendly chat, and for five minutes took all of Marberry's thrusts and lunges as though they had been made with a willow wand. I have never seen such a defense.

"I called to him at last: 'Clovelly, if you can finish this business, do so. The sun will be up anon.'

" 'Why,' says he in return, and he turns his head to me, at the same time picking off a double thrust in the air as though it were a ripened apple; 'why,' says he, 'I have not had an opportunity to exercise my sword for three days, and my arm needs work.'

"I thought at first that it was braggadocio, but he spoke as seriously as I now speak to you. Finally I saw two or three fellows riding over a hill in hot haste and I recognized them as friends of Marberry.

"I called again and told Clovelly that if he wished revenge, he must take it before the riders came up with us. He looked up to the top of the hill, at this, at the same time putting by a lunge as I might put by the importunate hand of a child.

" 'It seems that you are right,' says he, and then turns upon Marberry. It was, as I have said, a flash of lightning. A dazzle of light played before his face against which he offered a wild and vain defense. Then the small sword of Clovelly went clean through his body—"

"Gad!" breathed the duke.

"As he fell, Clovelly leaned and wiped his rapier upon Marberry's coat.

" 'In the name of God,' said I, 'you have killed him!'

" 'In the name of the devil,' said he, 'I wish I had, but I changed my mind at the last instant. However, Marberry will remain in his bed for some weeks and if he is bothered with indigestion hereafter, I shall not be surprised.' "

"A devil, not a man!" cried Ipswich.

"So I thought. But, as I said before, I was revenged upon Marberry."

"But what was the account of Cecily Medhurst."

"I am under oath not to speak of her."

"Oath to yourself?"

"To Clovelly."

"What the devil had he to say?"

"To him, the girl is no more than so much dirt. He is one of these fierce fellows who says that a woman tainted had better be a woman dead; she is worse than worthless, he says, for she corrupts the pure of her sex. Nevertheless, he seems to have an odd scruple about talking of her. He says that for a man to attack the reputation of a woman is like beating a child with a club. There is no possible rejoinder."

"Very apt, though very blunt. But is the fair Cecily indeed proven frail?"

"I cannot tell you, your grace. I have said that my word is pledged."

"And with Marberry?"

"Sir, I cannot ask you to continue guessing."

"However, it very aptly completes a picture of the affairs of the fair Cecily which I have just had from another source. Tell me, is she indeed half as fair as is rumored?"

"If she were as fair within as without," said Milverton, "she would be an angel of the purest grace. I say it without exaggeration; I have never seen anything so lovely or so lovable."

"I see that you were stung to the quick, my friend. Now let me show you another side of the picture. I have a letter here from an old friend of mine, Medhurst himself. Do you know him well?"

"I knew his brother, and through him I came to know Cecily."

"His brother was a Puritan, I believe?"

"He was."

"That gives me another link in the chain, then. However, since you do not know Medhurst, let me give you a short picture of the man. He is a cavalier of the oldest school. In his day, he might mutter against some of the ways of Charles the First, but after his death, he put two gods in heaven—the Creator and poor murdered Charles. And I think that he prays more often to the latter than to the former. So much for his religion.

"As for his manners, he is one that likes no horse which will not come rearing out of the stable and try to break its own neck and its rider's; he loves hunting so well that a good dog is dearer to him than a human friend; he talks much but he cannot speak without cursing.

"He damns his daughter while he praises her; I have always thought that he must have been damning his wife when he asked her to marry him. He carries a sword as high as his shoulder and a temper as short as his heel. He has fought in so many bloody duels and battles that he is a mass of scars from head to foot and a change in weather makes him groan with his old cuts.

"This is the good cavalier. You know his size and his bearing. As for virtues, it is said that he will die sooner than part with an old friend or let one perish for the lack of aid. The result is that he has always some half a dozen old companions hanging about his table, talking of hunting, drinking his ale, and fencing with him in the afternoons.

"He came to court at one time, but he fought so many duels within a fortnight that his gracious majesty had to give him private and kindly orders to return to his country estate, which, after all, was where the good fellow was happiest. And he was so overwhelmed by the gracious goodness of the first Charles in actually coming to him and speaking to him of his own affairs, that it is said he dropped upon his knees and thanked God for so kind a king and friend until he burst into tears and could speak no more.

"I have heard this story of his temper while he was at the court. He was sitting with a very old friend, a dear and tried companion, and they were arguing hotly together over some small point in hunting the stag. A mutual friend who passed them paused to hope that they were not quarreling, being such old acquaintances. 'Have no fear,' says Sir Egmond, who was the other of the pair, 'when my voice is loud I am least danger-ous. I never quarrel; I strike.'

"Up jumps Medhurst with fire in his eye.

" 'What?' says he. 'Strike? And strike me? You dare not—you dare not, Sir Egmond.'

" 'Who the devil has spoken of striking you, Hal?' demand-ed his friend.

" 'If there is striking on foot,' thunders the mad fellow, 'I hope that I am not the least forward man in the world!'

"With that he catches up his glove and strikes Egmond across the face. Directly the swords of the two are out, Medhurst raging and raving and Egmond wondering what in the devil it is all about. Presently Medhurst, who is a famous fighter, runs him through the thigh, a horrible wound, and Egmond goes down; whereat Medhurst sits by his bed night and day to nurse him and bring him back to strength.

"This will give you some conception of the fine old fellow if you do not know him closely. As for my acquaintance with him, his father was a friend of my father, and he himself, when I was a youngster, performed two or more great services for me, so that we became intimate. He detests my morals and my loose-living, but he cannot help but respect one who is a friend of the king."

Here Ipswich broke into laughter.

"But I shall read you his letter, since you opened the matter so far yourself that I am hardly betraying the confidence of the worthy cavalier.

" 'Dear George,' he read, 'being in a bad corner, between a wolf and a bear, as one may say, I am turning to you for help and for the comfort of good advice. You know that I have been recently in London where I have been prevented from calling upon you and offering my service to you by the known fact that you were carrying a heavy press of the business of the realm at this time.'

"There's a thrust for me," chuckled his grace. "The rascal can use the point as well as the edge, it seems."

He continued: " 'As for the reason of my leaving my country estate of Medhurst Park, to which his majesty, the late sainted Charles Stuart, with his own lips advised me to retire—' you mark, Milverton, that even in his excitement the good old man cannot leave out a reference to that affair—'I departed from the park for a sad and deep reason, it being that my daughter, Cecily, against all course of kind, had fallen into the puritanical, damned canting ways of my brother, with whom she lived those years while I was in exile together with all hearts who loved the fortunes of the king and his person more than their own affairs.

" 'My brother Tom, in short, had made her into one of his kind, and it was only with much ado that I could wean her half from those opinions when I returned at last to my estate. But when I thought that I had almost succeeded, I discovered that she was carrying on a secret correspondence with one of the foremost of the damned Cromwellians, a young rascal named Oliver Perth, of whom you may have heard. She had come to know him well, and after my return he was cunning enough to know that nothing could make me endure him, so that he induced her to meet him in private.

" 'I discovered this when I found her sending to him a locket in which I had had her miniature painted at great cost and on the back of the picture she had written her name and a foolish message of affection. I straightway took the thing, cross-examined her, discovered the state of her heart, and resolved to betroth her at once to some young man of the right blood and the right opinion.

" 'I looked about me, therefore, until I came upon young Lord Pennistone and invited him to my house, let him meet the girl, who is an enchantress, and then opened my thought to him, which was exceedingly much to the comfort of his heart, I assure you. Straightway I accomplished their betrothal and made Cecily give him the miniature with the message upon it with her own hand, though only through a threat that did she not do so, I should straightway drag her to the altar and see her married, if it were necessary to wring the responses from her by means of a whip—'"

"In the name of heaven," broke in Milverton, "do I hear these strange things rightly? Is this a modern man of the reign of Charles the Second, or is it some shag-haired barbarian out of the Russian wilderness?"

"This is a modern man," laughed Ipswich. "Consider the poor girl in such hands. If she erred at last, might she not have some excuse for it? But let's get on to the cream of this strange letter."

He cleared his throat, laughed at the prospect of what lay just before them, and began to read once more.

" 'I saw, however, that my daughter was in fact too deeply in love with the Roundhead, Oliver Perth, to be brought into a marriage with any hope of happiness, and so I bethought me of a way of solving the trouble.'

"What will you guess, Milverton, as to his way of solving the problem?"

"It is quite beyond me to guess. The man is a prodigy and not to be ordinarily estimated."

"He is not, I agree. But listen to this solution, as he calls it!"

CHAPTER XIV

GAME AFOOT

HE SHOOK HIS head, and continued with the reading of that strange letter: " 'It seemed clear to me, my friend, that my daughter's happiness might never be truly secured until I had disposed of her attachment to the Roundhead, and since it seemed to be a stubborn thing in her mind, and grew as if nourished by my opposition, I decided that I must discourage her in another way. In short, I decided to brush Perth out of the way, and to that end I sent a good friend of mine and a fine swordsman to encounter Perth and leave him where he might have the longer sleep.' "

"Murder!" cried Milverton.

"A broad word," answered the duke, "but not an inappropriate one. But he sees no wrong in his course. Listen to this:

" 'Because it seemed to me that the world would be certainly the better if there existed not a one of the accursed hypocrites and blood-letters who martyred the late blessed majesty of England. And if the world were better if they were all removed, certainly there was no blame attached to me if I removed one who was obnoxious above the rest to me.

" 'I sent out my friend the swordsman, as I have said—a man of peculiar graces with the sword far surpassing mine own, but to my great astonishment and discomfort, my friend was carried back to me with a thrust through his body, and bringing the word that Oliver Perth bore his sword as though the arch fiend had been his fencing master. I then bethought me of an old companion who had fought on the continent—a man of the greatest delicacy in fence although his arm had not sufficient strength to make him a cleaver of armor in battle.

" 'I sent for him and opened my heart to him, and he readily, for a small consideration, undertook to make away with Perth. He sallied out, accordingly, and my hopes were high, but he came back at the end of a day with two wounds, and with many oaths, saying that I had led him into a trap and brought him against some famous master who was living there in disguise.

" 'I was so enraged at this that I rushed out and flung myself upon a horse and galloped away to Perth's house where I encountered him, and had the great shame and the humiliation to find my sword taken from my hand by a sort of witchcraft of his blade, whereupon he told me that he spared my life because he hoped that I might some day be his father as well as the father of Cecily, which made my gorge so rise that I left him, being half blinded with shame and with scorn.

" 'After this, I could not directly attempt him, at once. So I took Cecily to London, knowing that the business of the Roundhead would not allow him to follow us on to town. And I was right. But other events having risen which make it necessary to go back to Medhurst Park, I have determined this time to make a great effort to rid myself of the neighborhood of Oliver Perth.

" 'To this end, I am opening my heart to your grace and I doubt not but that you will find some resolute blade who will come down to the country, rid me of Perth, and so take a burden off my heart, for I have sworn to see my daughter dead rather than married to a ranter. This shall be the reward of the man whom you shall send:

" 'I shall marry him to my daughter, will she or nill she. And as a result of that marriage, he shall have on the one hand the duty of making her obedient to his will and on the other hand he shall have the pleasure of inheriting my estate, which shall go to him utterly at my death, which I pray to God may not be long delayed but that He will deliver me out of troubles. Thine with an afflicted heart, Geoffrey Medhurst.'"

So ended this strange letter, and the two for a moment sat in silence, staring at each other, busy with their own thoughts and conjuring up the picture of the stern old cavalier which the letter had painted for them. It was Ipswich who laughed.

"I have more than half a mind to ride up country to the park and take this adventure on my own hands," he said. "But there is this disadvantage, that there is most bitterly pressing business at hand for me. And I dare not leave London for the moment. Alas, Milverton, life is no longer a happy game for me."

He sighed heavily as he spoke, and Milverton swallowed a smile, for he well knew that the incredible levity and reckless-ness of this man had more than once staggered the credit of the entire kingdom.

"But what of your friend, the invincible fencer, the thunder-bolt with the sword?" he asked Milverton, with something approaching a sneer.

"Marry such a creature?" said Milverton. "You cannot imagine with what a terrible scorn he spoke of her and of her kind. There will be no light of love in his life."

"What? What?" cried the duke, as one who could not com-prehend such a statement.

"My friend, Clovelly," said Milverton, "has odd fancies con-cerning women, and the oddest is his belief that just as all men love only one God, so all men should each love only one woman and make her a holy thing in their lives, a religious influence."

"The man is a saint, then."

"The man is a heart of ice and a hand of steel," said Milver-ton with a sort of solemn conviction. "Life and death are nothing in his eyes. I think he had as soon kill as breathe. But all men have one weakness, as I have heard your grace yourself announce more than once.

"And the weakness of Clovelly is this passion of his to find a woman, beautiful, wholly good; and I verily believe that he has traveled around the entire earth in search of nothing but such a creature. He has never yet found that for which he hunted and, therefore, he despises womankind. Yet he is so sensitive, that when he heard the voice of this girl, Cecily Medhurst, he told me that he grew faint with excitement, the quality of the tone was so lovely."

"She must be truly rare," said the duke to himself.

"She is more than rare; she is unique."

"This man of steel and ice—suppose that he were to marry her and bring her to London and, since he does not value her, sell the key to her apartments as another man would sell a horse?"

Milverton shuddered.

"It is a detestable thing," he said. "But I believe that Clovelly would actually do it. But to marry her, and then to give her away—I cannot tell."

"He would shrink from doing such a thing?"

"I cannot tell. Marriage, I think, means little as a rite or a vow to Clovelly. It is the woman that matters to him. 'I have only one regret,' he said to me about Cecily Medhurst, 'and that is that every tainted woman is not hanged by the neck until she be dead the instant that her taint is known to the world!'"

The duke raised his brows and considered his visitor, but it was plain that his mind was wandering far, far away.

"To kill Perth, marry the girl, bring her to London, and then, since he loathes her, leave her to the ministrations of one who is not so utterly abhorrent of those who have proved too tender, too fragile, to withstand their affections," said the duke at last, rising and beginning to walk up and down the apartment—"that, I presume, would not be impossible, my friend?"

"It is something, however, that I should not care to suggest to Clovelly in person."

"Send him to me. I fear no man, thank God; I would suggest a new fashion in horns to the devil if there were occasion. Go find Clovelly, Milverton, and send him at once to me."

Milverton arose, but slowly.

"It is a strange business, sir," he said, "and—"

"Come, Milverton, you are convinced that the girl is not honest?"

"There is no doubt about that. I have heard with my own ears."

"Then let us have no more talk. Send me Clovelly, and if he is the cold-blooded devil you say he is, the matter is as good as ended."

So Milverton left the room and went through the door, pausing every step or two as if he were struck by a new thought which was not quite worthy of making him turn to utter it.

"This is a hard burden for him to carry," said the duke to himself. "I believe that he is still half in love with this girl in spite of what he knows about her, and yet I think that very shame will now drive him on. Hello, Randal!"

The valet answered at once.

"I see no other person. If the king himself were to come, tell him the doctor bids me not be disturbed. Randal, I have game afoot!"

CHAPTER XV

A JACKAL'S TRICK

IT WAS A scant hour after this that Michael Clovelly entered the presence of the duke. He was no longer dressed in threadbare garments, but was attired in a short-waisted doublet and petticoat breeches, the lining being lower than the breeches and tied above the knees. The breeches were set off with ribbons; over the waistband hung his shirt, drawn outside so that its fineness might be the better observed.

He wore a high-crowned hat adorned with a tuft of feathers; lace ruffles showered about his hands, and a deep lace collar adorned the cloak which hung jauntily from his shoulders. He carried this elaborate costume with a natural dignity and an air of grace which astonished the duke, who had been prepared to encounter a bold blade and a hard-handed roisterer of the streets, not one with the exterior of a gentleman.

He received him, however, as if the stranger bore a title as great as his own. He saw to the chair in which Clovelly sat, so that it might not be too greatly turned to the light from the window; and he called for Rhenish wine, which he assured Clovelly was the only drink for the morning.

"I am under an oath," said Clovelly, "which prevents me from tasting wine or any liquor; but I thank your grace."

"Such an oath," declared his grace, "is a barbarous and medieval thing; and I had for my part rather be condemned to a year of exile than to a year without wine. What on this side of the devil's name could have made you take such an oath? But

I understand that you are a fellow of secrecy and that you rarely talk about yourself?"

"Not to others," answered Clovelly, "but to your grace I hope that I may be entirely open."

"I pray you, be so."

"The devil could not have forced that oath from me, but the accursed Spaniards did. I cannot drink until I am revenged."

His face grew so black that Ipswich watched him soberly.

"Tell me," he suggested gently.

"I shall paint a picture for you," said Clovelly, growing white with excitement as he talked. "Consider a man hanging upon a cross, tied by the wrists and the ankles to the posts.

"He has been there so long and the cords are so tightly drawn that they have cut through the skin and into the flesh, and blood trickles slowly. He is naked and you can see that his hands and his feet are purple with the stopped blood.

"He has fainted, but now he is wakened. The Spaniards thrust slivers of wood into his flesh and light them. The wood is pitchy and the splinters burn furiously until they are put out by the living flesh, and the smoke of that human body is horrible in the air."

"No more," said the duke hastily. "What? What? In this day? Such enormities?"

"They brought me to see this. I had been tortured the day before and they were keeping me until I had recovered enough strength to be tortured again. That was my father who hung on the crucifix, however, and they had brought me to torture me with this sight. They are very ingenious, my lord!"

"You overcome me with horror!"

"I am telling you this truth that you may understand why I want a certain price for my services."

"Since you are so frank, Mr. Clovelly, tell me what you understand those services to be?"

"I understand them very well. I am to kill Oliver Perth or so manage it that he is removed from the consideration of the girl. Then I am to marry her and bring her to your lordship in London where you will entertain her at your own expense."

He stated this in so calm a voice that even the duke, wild and debauched as his life had been, was staggered.

"You have nerves of steel, Clovelly!" he assured his companion.

The latter waved his hand.

"It is nothing," he declared. "If her soul were as clean as her voice is sweet, my lord, all the gold that the Spaniards have torn out of the earth in the Indies and all that they stole from Peru and Mexico would not be enough to bribe me to do this thing which we have in mind. But since there is a taint in her life, I swear to you, sir, that she is less to me than the horse I ride on."

He spoke this with such a magnificent contempt in his voice that the duke flushed to the hair with confusion. But Clovelly ran on smoothly enough to remove some of the sting from his words.

"But in such matters," he said, "I know that my opinion is not the opinion of the world. I say, however, that I shall be at your service, but remember this, my price is high."

"Name it, then."

"A ship of a hundred tons, at least, fully armed with the best cannon, with heavy store of powder and of shot, with muskets and ball in great stock, with cutlasses, and with some boxes of medicaments and a few sundries, together with enough ready cash to hire a crew that will run the good ship out to the Main."

His grace whistled softly.

"Do you consider," he said, "that a girl whom you with your own lips have just said is not worth so much as the horse that you ride upon could be possibly worth the great expense which you have just summed up for me?"

"It would be a loan, only," Clovelly asserted with a suppressed eagerness. "The value of that loan I am confident that I can repay and repay two-fold within a year's cruise."

"Or else rot at the bottom of the sea."

"Or else rot at the bottom of the sea," admitted Clovelly.

His calm manner made the duke smile.

"There will be bloodshed on the Main if ever you get there with such a company," he said. "How long ago did the wretches murder your father?"

Clovelly's face grew absolutely white.

"Eight years ago," he admitted at last in a husky voice.

His grace started. "Eight years? Is it possible!" he cried.

"Shame burns me!" said Clovelly huskily. "And I hasten to give some explanation. I am assured in my heart that I shall have what I want from your grace, and therefore, you shall learn everything you wish.

"I was at that time eighteen and I knew in my soul of souls that I had neither the experience of mind nor strength of body to attempt the things of blood which I had in mind.

"I determined not to move rashly against the Spaniards and so merely make myself a prey to them, but to wait until I had schooled myself and made myself a man; and some years were spent before I was satisfied that I was ready to do my best against them."

"But," said his grace, "your narrative left you in the hands of those fiends who murdered your father, and you were being held for further torture."

"They determined to turn me into service, however, and I was chained in their galleys for two years, after which I escaped and made my way to Europe."

"Two years at the sweeps? Can you dismiss such a torment in a mere phrase. And at eighteen! I thought that even strong, matured men died of the labor and the whips and the food."

"They do, but I had something to live for and would not die. I lived, and gained strength in my arms which will never leave me."

And he made a little gesture with his slender, bony hand which suddenly suggested to the duke all the power of a Hercules.

"When I reached Europe," said Clovelly, "I spent three years traveling from place to place and studying the art of fence. I had neither the length of arm nor the weight of shoulders to smash heads and cleave bodies like the buccaneers on the Main. I needed to learn adroitness, and I have done my best to acquire it.

"At the end of that time, I joined a crew of fellows bound for the Main, but at the start they changed their minds, dipped into the Mediterranean to pick up what they could there, and promptly fell in with half a dozen Moorish galleys during a calm. They ran us aboard and murdered the crew.

"I went down with half a dozen wounds, but lived and was sold into slavery again when I had recovered. I was three years in that condition, being with various masters and living with them in many places, from Morocco to the Ganges. But at last I escaped on a certain night—"

Here he paused a moment, and a gleam of savage satisfaction came into his eyes, so that the little silence meant more to his auditor than all that had been said before.

"And I came back to England, where I fell at last into an adventure which brought me to his grace of Ipswich, and that famous man, when I had served him, fitted me out with the ship and the arms which I required!"

As he said this, he leaned forward and watched the face of the duke carefully, and the latter nodded in spite of himself.

"You don't seem to be lucky," said his grace, "but I have bet a fortune on many a losing horse; and the race is no less exciting whether one wins or loses."

"I have not been lucky," Clovelly agreed, "from the one viewpoint. But from the other, I have nothing to be desired. These eight years have been a long and arduous school, but during them I have learned to become the master of myself and of my weapons. I have made my smallsword and my pistols a part of me and I have practiced with the muskets which after all, are the chief weapon of the buccaneers.

"I have seen all manners and all schools of fighting. I have studied scimitar work in Turkey and saber play in Poland, where they fight all day and drink all night. I have had the opportunity, also, to study men as well as weapons, and I begin to feel that when I walk the deck of my own ship, the men under me shall not be unwilling to obey my commands. Then, once on the Main, I may perhaps teach the Spaniards to know my name somewhat better than they knew the name of my father."

His hands were locked together with bone-breaking force, but he had himself under such perfect control that he was able to smile at Ipswich. And the latter, with a sudden oath, swore that he should have whatever he wished.

"Besides," he said with a new eagerness, "there is gold on those seas. Who can tell whether you would not make me a profitable partner?"

"I promise you that I have great hopes, your grace."

"Clovelly, give me your hand!"

They shook hands fervently.

"There will be no need of writing?"

"None!"

"Clovelly, I understand that you have returned, out of a foolish scruple, everything you took from Redbourne except certain sovereigns and the picture of the girl."

"It is here, sir." And he extended the miniature to Ipswich.

The duke studied it as if he were reading a book.

"By the eternal heavens!" he said to himself at last. And he called aloud: "Wine, Randal!"

Randal, who from a corner had heard everything with the ears of a fox, brought the wine at once, and as he served it, dipped the little locket from the pocket of his master. He retired presently outside the room to study the face, and as he stood in the passage a shadow fell suddenly across his feet.

He put the picture hastily behind him and confronted a tall man with a lean, swarthy-skinned, ugly face, and a half dozen cocker spaniels rolling and playing at his heels. Another was supported in the crotch of his arm.

"Tell George I must see him," said the tall man. "Go give him good morrow from me, Randal, and tell him that I am coming to open a scheme to him. Peace, Bess, silly thing," he added, stroking the silken head of the dog. "If the man has a wolfish look, he shall not hurt you, none the less."

Poor Randal was in the meantime sweating with anxiety.

"Your majesty," he said, "his grace is ill, and the doctor has forbidden him to speak with anyone. He lies in a darkened room," continued the valet, gathering warmth as he proceeded into the heart of lie, "and he seems most ill at ease."

The large, dark, and lack-luster eyes of Charles fixed steadily upon Randal. Then he smiled.

"What is the trinket you were studying, Randal?" he asked.

And he held out his hand. Randal quaked to his shoes, but oppose that command he dared not, and with trembling fingers he rendered up the miniature. His majesty surveyed it with an unmoved face, and then returned it to the valet.

"Is this the sickness of Ipswich?" he asked.

Randal rolled his eyes at the dark ceiling and then at the floor, but he found in neither place an answer written for him.

"I do not know," the miserable fellow replied.

"Come," said the king, smiling again, "you know a great deal if you will once open your lips to speak to me. And I must be spoken to, Randal. I intend to have this matter opened to the bottom—to the bottom.

"Come to me within the hour," he continued to Randal after an instant of thought. "Come and ask for Jessop. He will have word to bring you instantly before me. And in the meantime, not a syllable to his grace about my coming. Be wary, Randal, and great things may grow into your hand out of this adventure."

So, raising a forefinger in caution, he turned away and departed, with the spaniels still playing busily about his heels.

CHAPTER XVI

IMMURED

MY LORD PENNISTONE was as nervous as a boy attending school for the first day's work, and he eyed the imposing form of Medhurst with uneasy awe. He had been striving for some weeks to adjust himself to the thought of such a man as a father-in-law, but he had been unable to do so. And with each visit to the old cavalier, the young viscount felt more and more ill at ease.

"So early up! So early up!" cried Geoffrey Medhurst in his great voice as he entered the room where his visitor was waiting for him. "You have torn the new fashions to shreds and tatters, Herbert. You lounge in your bed till eleven and in your room over your toilet till noon. But what? Out on the road and ten miles away before prime?"

His guest smiled without enthusiasm.

"Of course," he said, "when I learned that Cecily and you had returned to the park, I hurried over at once to pay my respects, sir."

"A thousand thanks. Have you had your morning draft?"

"With your leave, sir, I wish to have my wits about me when I see Cecily."

"So? So?" replied the cavalier, with perhaps a touch of contempt in his tone. "But I must not drink alone. I have a vow against doing so. Wet your throat with one swallow."

He looked about him, saw no ready means of calling a servant by a bell, and therefore beat against the wall with the flat of his hand, making the stout partition shudder under the heavy strokes. He called for ale for himself and wine for his guest when the servant appeared.

And he ran on carelessly about the last stag hunt in which he had ridden, until the drink arrived. Then he pledged Pennistone in a mighty potion which appeared to give him great comfort, for he leaned back in his chair and eyed his lordship with a fixed gravity.

"What is news with you?" he asked.

"Of no importance. But I wish particularly to inquire is Cecily—"

Medhurst broke in as if he had not heard the latter part of this speech.

"No news? What, have they not yet secured that infamous rascal who stopped the coach after it had entered your own grounds?"

"They have not, to my knowledge."

"A daring, wild-riding knave. He jumped the big wall, I hear."

"He did, sir."

"And without giving his horse a run at it, either."

"He took it sidling, I believe. It was a great jump."

"I have seen better—I have seen better; but for these days it was well enough done. In the old times, men rode. Nowadays they only canter. A hunt to-day is a parade, not a ride. Hell of fire, they breed skinny horses and lesser men, I begin to think."

"It may be so, sir," said Pennistone, and his glance turned in haunted fashion toward the great door through which Cecily must at any moment surely appear.

"But in the meantime, where has the trail led?"

"It was not surely followed. People think that it was from London. Others differ."

"They'll spot him by the horse. A monster, was it not?"

"I myself thought it was a full seventeen hands. Sir Christopher, from the coach, made it out to be no more than sixteen hands. It was quite dusk, and we were in an excitement."

"But at least the color is odd enough to catch eyes. It was a milk-white horse, I believe."

"As white as snow."

"Without dark points?"

"I believe not. The impression of all of us was that the horse was shining white."

"Well, I put small faith in one of those damned albinos. There's sure to be a weakness in 'em somewhere, Pennistone. What of the rider?"

"I thought he was a man of middle size, rather slender than otherwise. But Sir Christopher felt him to be a full six feet, at the least, and Lady Redbourne believes that he was even larger—larger than you, sir, but I am confident that he was not."

"A mixed description. No wonder that they have not yet found him. If you could agree no better than that on the man, there's nothing to hunt for but a milk-white horse."

"I think that the hunt has ended, sir. The strangest part of the whole adventure is the sequel to it. The day before yesterday the entire body of the plunder was returned to Sir Christopher with the exception of sixty pounds and the locket.

"And this very morning the sixty pounds missing and the locket were brought back together with a most courteous note in which the robber regretted that a temporary necessity had forced him to borrow our possessions, but stated that he had met his need in another way and was using his first opportunity to return to us what was ours.

"He also regretted the blow with which he had struck me down, but pointed out that if he had not done so, he must have shot me point-blank, which would have been death."

"The devil fly away with me!" thundered Medhurst. "This is more like a page out of a story than facts."

"This, however, is a fact," said his lordship joyfully, and he exposed the recovered locket.

The eye of Medhurst darkened when it fell upon the face.

"And I wonder," said the viscount with a touch of irritation, "if Cecily has been told that I am here?"

"She is ill," said Medhurst hastily, and looking down to the floor. "She is ill, my lord, and cannot see you."

He had spoken in such a manner that it was plain that he stated only a portion of the truth. And the viscount sat bolt upright, staring, and sickly white.

"She's ill," said Medhurst, and then blurted out, as if he could not endure to inflict a sham reason upon his guest, "and the fact is, my lord, that there has come about a great change in plans. I fear, sir, I greatly fear that she will not marry you."

His lordship steadied himself by gripping the high arms of a chair which had been built for the ample bulk of Medhurst, and which, therefore, was by far too large for him.

"I am ready to understand you, sir, if I can," he said, gravely

"Damn it, boy—damn it, Herbert," groaned the big man. "This is torment to me—but in a word, her mind was so fixed upon the damned Roundhead, that I could not drag it away. There's only one way to marry her, and that's to get rid of the Puritan first. Pennistone, if you give me word that Oliver Perth is dead, I think that the marriage may be still brought about."

With this, he sat a moment staring at the agonized face of the young viscount until he could endure it no longer, and then he arose and fled like a child from a mischief which it has done. As for the viscount, he finally managed to stagger from his chair and to leave the house. But on the way through the woods, he encountered an old servant of the house who also was a fast friend of his own.

"Jarvis," he said, suddenly drawing rein, "what have they done with Mistress Cecily?"

The fellow had touched his cap and he now dragged it off so that his coarse hair stood on end and his startled eyes blinked up at the rider.

"God knows, your lordship," he said, "what's wrong in the

house. There's a whispering and a talking going on. Mr. Medhurst says that she's sick. But there's some in the kitchen that
says she's as well as ever she was."

"Is it possible?" murmured the viscount, and he turned and
stared toward the house.

"Where does she lie—sick?"

"In the old western tower, sir."

It loomed high about the rest of the sprawling building, a
great gray Norman keep, the edges rounded by the moldering
of time.

"What can it be?" he asked himself, but Jarvis answered as
if the question were put to himself.

"It means the end of the happy times in the park, sir," he said
dolorously.

The viscount rode gloomily on his way. They had imprisoned
Cecily, he decided, to keep her from running away with the
Roundhead. What should his own course of action be?

CHAPTER XVII

BEWARE THE KING

A BRISK RAIN had fallen the night before, and the roads quickly became quagmires. For they were alternately either a foot thick in dust or else a wash with liquid mud, which, hardening a little, the wheels rutted tremendously deep.

And such a road as that from London to Oxford, over which there was a constant coach service, was tremendously bad. At all seasons, the coaches required two days for a run of well under sixty miles. And this was considered fast service.

As for Clovelly, he was a hard and steady rider, yet when he had compassed forty miles of his journey up-country, he decided that he had done enough for that stage, and turned into a wayside inn with his white horse converted into a black one with the mud and he himself splashed from head to foot; for White Harry was a mighty goer, and when he trod in a small puddle he cast up a spray that fairly drained the spot.

But Clovelly made nothing of such traveling, or such weather. He had burned under the open sun in the stifling and filthy waist of a galley on the Spanish Main with sweating, groaning negroes lashed to the other sweeps; he had labored into the dreary north over the steppes, so that the extremes of temperature which he had endured as a slave meant nothing to him now that he was a freeman.

Before he even thought of cleansing himself of the marks of travel, he looked first to the comfort of White Harry and tended him with such pains that the ostler stood about to gape at him;

he bedded Harry comfortably down, groomed him, and looked to his feed, that it be neither too much nor too little, for White Harry, like all good horses, was a pig, and would gorge himself like a child among sweetmeats if he had a chance.

He left Harry wallowing his head deep in the hay in his manger and paying small heed to the angry snorts of an ill-natured gelding which occupied the neighboring stall. Then the master went to his room, cleansed himself, came down for a prodigious supper of cold meats unmoistened with liquor, and sat afterward smoking a single pipe without a word to any one, and finally went off to his bed.

But he went to rest like a prisoner spending a first night in a new prison. He took off his boots so that his movements would be noiseless, and after that he roamed around the room with no more sound than a shadow. He examined the walls, the ceiling, which was low enough for him to touch, the great bed, and the floor beneath it.

Over the floor he went with a particular caution and then looked out the window. It opened upon a lower roof some three feet beneath it, the roof of the penthouse which served as the ceiling of the kitchen. He made this examination without apparent emotion and with such speed that it showed he considered it a merely ordinary precaution. He seemed to be thoroughly satisfied now with the condition of the room, only opening the window a little wider.

Next he took a sliver of wood and forced it down into a crack between two boards and near the door so that if the door were opened the bit of wood must be broken.

Last of all, he took a sponge bath, re-donned his clothes, and having first laid his boots near the window, he lay down upon the bed with his pistols in his coat and his sword at his side. He had made such preparations as though he expected to be under the most deadly siege that night, but his head no sooner touched his pillow than he was sound asleep, and an emperor surrounded with a thousand guards could not have reposed with a greater seeming confidence.

He did not waken for a considerable time. It was hardly nine in the night when he closed his eyes. It was perhaps three in the morning when he was wakened by a light, snapping sound.

When he opened his eyes, he did not require time in which to come to his senses. He was not half drugged with weariness, but having slept with the profound relaxation of an animal, he awakened like a beast of prey. He opened his eyes, and it was as if he had never closed them. His thoughts instantly took up at exactly the point where they had left off the night before.

He knew what that cracking sound, slight as it was, had been; the sliver which he had planted before the door had cracked. He now made the only motion which a person lying flat in a bed can make and be sure of starting no noise.

He lifted his head without stirring foot or hand and stared intently at window and door. The window was empty; in the upper half of its rectangle there was a frame of half dozen stars; but when he glanced to the door he saw that it stood ajar.

He began to move with the greatest possible celerity to raise himself from the bed without making more than a whisper of noise. He had lain down close to the edge of that bed, or otherwise he could never have accomplished his desire, but a rattling gust blew up in the midst of his effort and before its murmur passed on over the house Clovelly was on his feet. He gripped the handles of his pistols, but then, with a wicked smile, he changed his mind and took out the naked sword.

He began to move across the room. And having tested the boards of the floor the night before with his weight as he walked, he appeared to have charged a map of the apartment in his mind. For he stepped from place to place like a man crossing a little river from stone to stone.

He raised his feet with even more care than he put them down, and when he placed them, the foot came down slanting, the outer edge striking at once and then the foot rolling inwards.

These seemingly complicated maneuvers Clovelly made with the smoothest fluid ease and at length was close to the door.

This, having swung ajar, remained for a moment motionless. Then it swayed wider and a head appeared looking inside. Clovelly was flattened against the wall with his sword tucked behind him so that no light might glint along its blade of bright steel.

The fellow who had peered in, presently stepped forward and there was the faintest of creaks from the floor as another glided behind him to enter. Then Clovelly acted.

It was not the point of the blade which he used, although he grimaced in the darkness with eagerness to be at his prey. Instead, he struck with the heavy pommel.

The blow landed behind the first interloper's ear, and Clovelly then cast his weight against the door. It struck a yielding object; there was a muffled exclamation and then two heavy footbeats as the man staggered back into the hall.

Clovelly dropped the bolt in place and turned to the first victim. The fellow was now a black splotch of shadow heaped upon the floor. He took him by the collar and dragged him to the bed, lifting a bulky body with surprising ease in his meager arms, and then lighted the candle.

He saw a big, raw-boned man, with a face whose hair had been trimmed to increase a natural ferocity of expression. His very eyebrows had been plucked so that they pointed upward and outward and his beard and mustaches had been trained to demoniacal points.

His expression even as he lay there unconscious was devilish. He was apparently as much awake as a cat that closes its eyes while it toys with a poor mouse, only waiting for the victim to move before it sprang.

But Clovelly tied the hands of his captive behind his back, secured his feet likewise, and strolled to the window in time to see a man come over the edge of the roof and then draw up a fellow after him. They flattened themselves against the thatch and began to work upward like snakes.

Clovelly was instantly at work. He laid his rapier aside. He drew out in its place a long and curved knife that looked like a small scimitar.

The two had paused to look up, cautiously, and then lowered their faces and crept on. At this, he lay out on the sill of the window, extended the knife, and as the foremost of the two felt the shadow of danger and glanced up, Clovelly slashed him straight down the face.

The edge was so sharpened that the blade rivaled a razor. It split the nose, the mouth and the flesh of the man's chin as if these were made of paper rather than flesh, and the poor fellow, clapping his hands to his ruined features, rolled down the roof with a stifled groan and landed heavily on the ground below. His companion gave Clovelly a single wild look and then leaped after his leader.

But there was no outcry. A stifled and inarticulate cursing sounded beneath the kitchen wall, but apparently even the agony of that dreadful knife slash was not as great to the wounded man as the fear of being discovered. Clovelly sat on the sill of the window and mused upon .this while he cleaned his knife in the thick thatch.

Than he put the grisly weapon away and went back to his captive, turning his back upon the window as securely, now, as though he had a dozen guards there, armed to protect him. He found that his prisoner was looking up with bright, inhuman eyes.

"Are you well?" said Clovelly not unkindly. "Does your head ache?"

The other stared at him without making a sound. So Clovelly filled a glass with water, brought it to his man, and lifted the latter's head so that he might drink.

"Having wet your whistle," he told his man, "you may as well tell me your story."

The other regarded him with an expression more unhumanly owl-like than ever and said not a word. Clovelly, therefore, studied him with the most perfect calmness for a moment, and then went to the chimney place at the side of the room. A fire had been laid and he took up some of the kindling until he found a stick rich with hardened rosin as clear-colored as amber. He struck a sliver off from this and approached his prisoner.

"Consider this, my friend," he said. "If I fix this splinter in your shoulder and then light it, it will burn down to the flesh in a short time and keep on burning until the flesh itself has smothered it."

His captive heard this speech with a sudden change of color, or rather a loss of it, but he thrust out his jaw, and although the sweat stood upon his forehead, he still did not answer with a syllable. After this Clovelly snapped the splinter across the room.

"Besides," he said, as if he were arguing with himself, "I cannot endure the stench of it."

He drew a cord from his pocket, tied it in a noose, and passed the noose around the head of his victim. Next, he passed one of the sticks of kindling wood through the open end of the loop and began to twist. It tightened at once.

"You understand?" said Clovelly.

The owl-like eyes regarded him without a quiver of expression. So Clovelly turned again. The cord drew murderously tight. He turned again. The cord sank into the flesh. He turned again, and the eyes of the captive started from his head.

"Ah," he breathed.

Clovelly instantly relaxed the strain; there was a little streak of blood across the forehead of the tortured man.

"I am glad that you changed your mind," said Clovelly. "Because I give you my word, friend, that if it were necessary, to make you speak, I'd keep turning until your eyes rolled out upon your cheeks."

He said it without overemphasis, with a deadly poise which

gave all that he said an added weight. His prisoner closed his eyes for a moment, overcome by the weakness of the reaction, and the hot agony of the pressure which had just left his head.

"What is it?" he said at last.

"The name of him who sent you."

"Clovelly, do not ask!"

"No?"

"If you know, you will saddle your horse and flee for the coast and get into a ship and never return to England while you live."

"Tush!" murmured Clovelly. And he began to walk up and down the apartment.

Suddenly he said: "The king!"

And he whirled upon the other. He found him staring at the ceiling.

"The king!" whispered Clovelly, bringing a face as savage as that of an Indian close to his prey.

"Yes," said that wretched man; "and if it is known that I have spoken, you are but a dead man, and I am but a dead man. He is a kind man when he chooses, but he is a devil incarnate, also, when he chooses. Clovelly, saddle your horse and fly!"

Clovelly walked to the window and considered the darkness of the night. There was no doubt that he was shaken to the very core of his being, and when he turned to the other, he was once and twice on the verge of speaking, but he each time changed his mind.

At length, he pulled on his boots, equipped himself with his small packet of belongings, and passed from the room. He paused at the door of the host and passed under it enough money to pay his score twice over. Than he stole down the stairs, through the heavy door, after he had unbarred it with the greatest of care, and finally out to the stable.

When he reached the stable door, he paused before he stepped into the dense wall of the blackness before him, but there was nothing else for it, and now White Harry caught the scent of his dear master and whinnied softly out of the gloom.

Clovelly went on and encountered no immediate danger. They had hunted him everywhere save in the place where he would be the least able to guard himself.

He found the big stallion, saddled him, and rode him out under the stars. There was not a sound from the inn as he passed it. The heavy thatch curved warmly about the dormer windows, the panes, like great black diamonds, glimmered at him, and there was only a trailing wisp of smoke from the great central chimney.

He passed under the arch of the wall and out into the open road. The stars were bright enough to show their faces in the dark little pools of water which stretched up the road. It was bitter work for him, it was bitterer work for White Harry.

But now the king rode against him and he had no time to waste, for the king could ride with ten thousand horses. And now the king's hand was raised against him, and the king's hand was ten thousand hands.

CHAPTER XVIII

THE TOWER OF FAITH

EVERY HOUR OF the sickness of Cecily Medhurst was becoming more and more strange to the servants in the house, for it was noted that no physician was called in to visit her, and her seclusion in the tower was made more and more complete. Neither was there anything to indicate that she was ill, although the diet which the master of the house said had been prescribed for her was very light. After the first three days, moreover, she was taken out for a walk each evening by Medhurst himself, and they strolled through the grounds of the park.

But though he planned these walks for the sake of keeping his daughter in good health and that the continued confinement might not make her desperate, yet the excursions were the worst part of the torment to Cecily. For not a word was ever spoken when she was out with her tall father.

He strode on with her, walking just half a pace to the rear and acting as if his sword was constantly ready to come from its scabbard to defend himself in case a surprise attack might be made upon him. Once or twice she had attempted to speak, but always her voice ended in a sigh, and the promenade was completed in speechlessness.

But they advanced on the third of these excursions to a hill near the edge of the estate. The trees had been cleared from its top and they commanded a clear prospect of the town. Each house, for the night was without mist, was plainly marked by its lights. Suddenly Medhurst spoke.

"What house do you look toward, Cecily?"

She did not answer for a moment, she was so taken by surprise. But finally she said bravely enough: "I am looking toward the house of my friend, Oliver Perth."

"I knew it," he told her without passion. "But do you think, Cecily, that your friend Oliver is looking toward you?"

"I hope that he is," she told him.

"Suppose," he said, "that I have told him the truth about Marberry?"

She gasped.

"What then, Cecily?"

She merely shook her head.

"Oliver knows me too well. He would not doubt me. He would not hold such a horrible thought against me for an instant. And such a thought as that—oh, never!"

"You are sure, girl?"

"I am a thousand times sure."

But her voice shook, as much as to say that she could not fortify herself with conviction strong enough.

"Does it not seem strange to you, Cecily, that he has not come to inquire after you?"

"He knows that it would be risking his life to put a foot on this estate, sir. He knows, surely, that you hate him."

"I hope that the Roundhead dog does!" thundered the cavalier, but he added, controlling his voice again: "But suppose that, in the old days, your mother had been fenced away from me by an angry father. What would I have done?"

She strove to conjure up the picture, but the thought of her mother being kept from the man who loved her could make her summon up nothing but pictures of blood and death.

"It would have been a terrible thing," she said.

"Do you think that mere walls of stone could have kept me away from her? Do you think that a damned old flimsy tower like the one yonder could have kept me out? I would have had it in ruins in a trice, and my dear out of the wreck and away with me over the hills. 'S blood, Cecily, I was not a creature made of milk and water in those days, though time has tamed me now—time has tamed me now."

And he sighed prodigiously.

"But your dear friend Oliver!" he said, with a ridiculous attempt to imitate the somewhat nasal utterance of that worthy. "He has not risked himself, God wot! He has sat fast at home and waited for news of you of another's bringing. Why, damn his cold heart! Even such as you are, my girl, even stained and worthless in my eyes now as a broken mirror, one fragment of you is still worth more than that dog shall have! Bah!"

He roared out his anger at the thought.

"I shall tell you a secret," he said, "to make your stay in the tower the happier. The man who pricks yonder rascal through the lungs, shall have you. I have let it be known, that the man who does away with Oliver Perth, shall have you as a reward!"

"No, No!" cried Cecily. "You dare not do so terrible a thing!"

"Dare not?" thundered her father. "Why I have dared not have *you* done away with and tossed into a grave, God alone knows. Why I allow your shame to live on, to break my old heart, I cannot tell. Dare not? Odds fish, fool, what I dare you cannot guess—you cannot guess! And you have put me in a humor for drinking blood! Marberry still lives. I have not forgotten that,"

Cecily dropped to her knees.

"In the name of heaven!" she pleaded. "Do him no harm, for he was innocent of any wrong with me. Name any oath for me to swear—I'll swear it."

Her father was stifled with rage and shame.

"Peace!" he gasped at length. "Peace and stand up! Oh shameless, to plead for your lover to my face—and such a damned lecher as the whole town of London knows him, and his name is like a taint to the ears of all decent citizens. To have sinned was enough, but to have sinned with such a man—oh God, what have my sins been to bring this on my head!"

He was silent for a moment, and Cecily arose slowly to her feet and leaned one hand against the trunk of a tree. She was half-fainting, but had she fallen dead with grief—had her swelling heart broken indeed—she knew that the only emotion of her father would have been one of joy that the end of her had come. And the horror of that thought somehow supported her.

"As for the Puritan," continued the cavalier, "he'll be rotting in his grave before the week is over. He has done well enough against ordinary blades, but I am sending for those who will end him before steel had tapped three times against steel—the rat!"

And with this bitter comfort, he took her back to the house, closed her again in the little square room, and turned the huge lock. She listened to his departing footfalls, she noted how he paused frequently on the stairs and in the hall beneath, stopped by the bitterness of his thoughts.

But as for Cecily, she sat for a long time with her elbows resting on the broken stonework which formed the bottom of the casement and her face resting in her hands. To leap through that window would bring her in a small, small fraction of a breathing space, to the end of all of her troubles.

Twice and again she half rose for the effort; and it seemed to her, as she sank back into her chair, that the words of her father had been true, after all. It was weakness of heart in Oliver Perth which had kept him from her in the time of her need.

Here something stung her forehead, and a piece of paper wrapped around a small pebble dropped upon the rock before her. She leaned out and looked down. A weak sickle of a moon was sliding through the western trees and by that light she saw clearly enough the figure of a man at the foot of the tower, forty feet below, waving toward her.

Was it Oliver Perth? Her heart leaped at the thought, and stepping back, she opened the missive.

"Cecily, my dear," she read as she unfurled the bit of heavy paper and the pebble tinkled against the floor. "Write on the paper only a word, and I shall have you out of the tower in spite of all the world. Only say that you are kept there against your will, and I shall have you out. And wherever you wish to be taken in the world, there you shall go, at your wish and not at mine own. But if you have nothing for which you can use me, then throw back the pebble to me without the paper and I shall know that you are contented to stay where you now stand."

And the signature was that of Herbert Theale, the lord of Pennistone! And the sudden thought came sickeningly home to her: What if her father had been right after all in his estimates of Oliver Perth, and what if Oliver had only a love for her estate and not for herself?

Then, sick at heart because she had even dared for an instant to doubt him, she started up and caught the pebble from the floor and dropped it through the casement. She could see Pennistone start. He looked about him, and then, realizing that only a pebble and not a message had been dropped, he turned away and went with a bowed head across the field and into the dark of the woodland.

CHAPTER XIX

TO SERVE THE SUMMONS

CLOVELLY STAYED NO longer in inn or taverns along the way to Medhurst Park, or rather to the town near by it. If the king's men had so nearly taken him in the beginning of his ride, they would set many a trap for him on the rest of his journey so long as he kept straightforward along the road as he had begun.

That was by no means his intention, however. He swung aside from the main highway and continued throughout that morning and the early part of the afternoon to ride toward his goal. In mid-afternoon he reached the town and found the house of Oliver Perth.

It looked like a Puritan's habitation. It was built perfectly square, of new gray stone, which promised to endure forever unless it were pulled down by his neighbors because its harsh face ruined the mellow beauty of the rest of the village street with curving lines of thatch, and moldering walls of soft yellow sandstone.

Clovelly looked up and down this street for a moment as he stood beside his panting horse, patting White Harry's nose. It had been a terrible journey, and White Harry had performed nobly; to the very end his driver had been forced to keep a tight rein, and even now, dripping and blackened with sweat, the noble stallion kept his head high and looked down the street with a far-off eagerness as if he yearned to be on toward a still more distant goal.

Then the master regarded the house of Oliver Perth. Whereas the rest of the town seemed drowzing along its winding street, the house of Perth presented a brisk and wide-awake face to the day. One could smell even from the outside, as it were, the prosperous and shining newness of the furniture.

When Clovelly rapped with the knocker, an empty echo passed with a hollow and mournful progress through the hall and down the stairs, but at length a woman opened the door. She was the type which Clovelly easily could have suspected as the servant of a Roundhead.

Her middle age gave promise of developing into the features of a very witch before she had passed through another ten years. Her form was wide and squat. The sharp slope of her forehead was partly masked by her hair, which began to grow only immediately behind her eyebrows.

Her face was built like a side of a pyramid, the jaw thrusting out and each feature above retreating; but the back of her head was well-nigh a straight line up and down. This repulsive creature was made formidable by the appearance of arms as long and as brawny as those of a hard-worked man.

She regarded Clovelly with a gloomy intentness, running her eyes boldly up and down his body. It could be seen that she loved the world no more than the world loved her.

"What will ye have?" she asked.

"A word with Mr. Perth."

"You must e'en wait," said she. "Are ye from Bristol?"

"No," said Clovelly.

She almost closed the door, as if this answer disposed of her last interest in him.

"You must e'en wait. Mr. Perth is out."

"I must find him soon. In what direction has he gone?"

"Follow your nose!" said the hag gloomily, and slammed the door.

He had a furious desire to smash down the door and drag her out to the ducking pond.

"If she were on shipboard, now," he muttered to himself—and then chuckled maliciously. It could be seen that there was little mercy in that lean face of his; there was no more tenderness in his soul than there was fat on his body.

"But," he said finally to himself, "since the townsfolk cannot or will not tell me where he is, I shall take it for granted that he has ridden out of town, and since he is not on the road over which I have just gone, I shall ride on through the village."

This he did, only to come a hundred yards from the last house upon a forking of the way. He hesitated, then shrugged his shoulders. At least he had diminished his chances of coming upon Oliver Perth by fifty per cent.

He pushed straight on to the left, with White Harry galloping as strongly and lightly as though his work for the day was barely beginning; for he was a creature of iron. The long days at the plow and at the cart had given him marvelous endurance, and a five minutes' blow made him ready to turn from one long run to another.

In half a mile the way divided to the left and at this Clovelly gave up all hope. He took the right hand way out of mere freak of fancy, and had pushed ahead for a scant ten minutes when the road doubled back upon itself as it swerved down the steep side of a hill, and Clovelly heard a sudden shouting, the explosion of a pistol or two, immediately followed by the familiar ringing of steel against steel.

From the edge of the way he looked down the hill and saw in the middle of the lower road—which was a scant fifty yards away—a tall man standing beside the dead horse, which must have been shot from under him, and engaging the swords of no less than three antagonists. They gave him their points in scattering fashion, but he picked off their efforts with the greatest address, using a small sword with a triangular blade like Clovelly's, although with a longer and somewhat heavier sweep.

Opposed to him were three rough-and-ready fighters who handled cut and thrust weapons of the usual length and clum-

siness. They drew back after the first assault, however, and came on again shoulder to shoulder and thrusting all at once. No adroitness of parrying could avoid all of those blades.

The tall man, who had the advantage of very long legs and extremely agile ones, dodged this danger by leaping a great distance to one side so that the thrusts of two of the men were sped into the thin air. The effort of the third man, nearest to him, he turned with his weapon and then plunged the small sword into that enemy.

There was a yell of dismay and rage from the latter, who dropped his rapier and clutched the left arm, into which the point of the other had entered. But the battle was by no means over. The two remaining warriors, who seemed the hardier and the more expert with their weapons, came eagerly at the tall man, still lunging in unison so that he had to trust his speed of foot for a full half of his defence.

Yet he fought with the greatest appearance of confidence, with a sort of sneering superiority of manner which took from Clovelly half of the admiration with which he had been watching the combat. Indeed, he was rather like some venomous snake circling slowly around a pair of barking dogs, uncertain when his time would come, but feeling that in the end he would have at them with his fangs, and in those fangs was death. He managed his small sword in that fashion, keeping it reserved like a terrible and impending danger which would not be launched except to strike a man dead.

And to Clovelly, who had a sense for sword play like that of a musician for music, the actual danger seemed to be on the side of the two rather than on the side of the tall man. But here another complexion was put on matters, for the bushes were thrust aside and two men came out directly behind the tall man.

At this, the two assassins redoubled their attack, driving him back toward their reinforcements. The latter, being armed with both pistol and sword, maneuvered toward the sides from which they might fire without endangering their friends who conducted the war from the front.

And it was now that Clovelly, who had sat as a calm, and almost as an indifferent observer of the brawl up to this point, came into action. He drew one pistol from his breast, aimed it almost negligently, and fired. One of the newcomers straightway pitched upon his face and then lay yelling upon the ground, clutching the leg through which the soft leaden bullet had torn its way.

The scene instantly became changed. The tall man at a glance marked the rescue and then leaped into punish his assailants while he had this aid at his back. But they had no mind to stand their ground. One of their men was cursing and striving to bandage his injured left arm down which the blood was running. Another lay prostrate and helpless on the ground.

And for the rest, the odds were now three against two instead of five against one. They retreated instantly, but in good order. Two made a sudden and violent attack upon the tall man, who retreated, calling out upon Clovelly to come to his assistance, and snare some of the rascals.

In the meantime, him of the wounded arm and the fourth assailant, ran to the man upon the ground, lifted him, and bore him into the brush. The last two then retreated, keeping a steady face to the tall man as he followed until they were among the brush. He hesitated only a moment and then plunged with great gallantry into the shadows. Clovelly still sat his saddle, however, and began to busy himself with the reloading of his pistol.

Now the tall man came forth again, but this time leading a big black horse which he had apparently captured from the marauders. He stripped the body of his own mount of the saddle and other trappings which it had worn, and securing them behind the cantle on the black, he swung into the stirrups and trotted up to join Clovelly, who had now finished the work of loading, which was performed with the most exacting care.

"Well," said Clovelly, as the other came toward him, "I think you have made a good exchange; yonder bay you were riding was an old horse and a bit long in the legs; but this black is a Hercules, and able to keep a good round pace on the road, as well, I warrant you."

"Young man," said the tall one, as he drew rein near his rescuer; "young man," he repeated with gloomy emphasis, although he could not have been more than two or three years senior to Clovelly, "why did you not press in and so take me from the great danger in which I stood? Besides which, they should not have escaped scathless."

"Scathless?" murmured Clovelly. "That fellow will have a bad time with his left arm. The sword point struck the bone squarely and perhaps bit a piece out of it."

"How could you tell that?" asked the tall man sharply.

"I saw your sword blade shiver in the middle of the thrust, and I knew the point was against bone."

"Ah!" said the other, and he again cast one of his keen glances at his new companion. Clovelly now found him to be dressed in the plainest but the best cloth, with heavy boots of cowhide, and his shirt plain white, with a short, stiff white collar. His hat was a piece with the rest of the dress, being high crowned and with a wide, stiff brim.

He was quite handsome, and his face was sobered but not marred by a perpendicular wrinkle between his eyes, a mark of seriousness of disposition. Clovelly regarded him with as much interest as he was himself examined, though less bluntly than the stranger conducted his investigation.

"And there was another," continued Clovelly, "who went down with a pistol bullet through his leg. Besides which they have lost a horse worth three of that one of yours which they shot. In addition to which you have had a brisk bit of exercise; and have paid for all with only that scratch under your right armpit."

He enumerated these things half seriously and half with a smile. But the tall man scowled and shook his head.

"I verily believe," said he, "that you stood above and enjoyed the combat for a game."

"I did," admitted Clovelly, "after I saw the first of the three go down, for I knew, as you knew, that the other two were in your hand, and that the instant they separated from the side of each other, you would run them through in a trice."

The stranger looked gloomily upon him and said nothing for a moment, but his flush showed that he was very angry. And Clovelly regarded him curiously. Here was a strange fellow whose life he had saved and who did not bother to thank him for that small gift.

"My name," said he, "is Michael Clovelly."

"My name," said the stranger, "is Oliver Perth."

"Ah!" said Clovelly. "Then you are my man. I have been riding to find you."

"Indeed?"

"With a most secret message. I can give it to you when we reach your house."

"Very good, sir. You are from—"

"Bristol."

"Ah! Ah!" The brows of the other were lifted.

"Let us push on," he said, in haste. "I am all eagerness to hear your news."

CHAPTER XX

PERFUME OF THE SEA

THEY RODE BRISKLY on for a time, with Clovelly wondering what the news could be from Bristol for which Oliver Perth was so eagerly waiting. And, in the meantime, he was deciding that he disliked this fellow as much as any man he had ever encountered in the course of his life.

He had never before met one from whom such a strong aroma of self-satisfaction and self-centered brooding exuded. And, little as he liked Perth, he felt that the man could be trusted even less.

It was strange, indeed, that such a man could have won the affection of a laughing girl like Cecily Medhurst. He was in the midst of these reflections when his companion drew up his horse and Clovelly was forced to follow suit.

"That was a rare shot," said Perth. "At fifty yards it was a rare shot, and a lucky one."

"It was not lucky," protested Clovelly.

"Ah! At least it was aimed for his body, not his leg."

"It was aimed for his leg," insisted Clovelly.

The other scowled for a moment in disbelief, but he was watching Clovelly with a greater and a greater interest.

"Leaving the marksmanship to one side," said he, "why would you not shoot to kill? Have you, perhaps, conscientious scruples against the slaughter of your fellow men?"

"Scruples," laughed Clovelly, "are pleasant things enough to cart about ashore, but they clutter up the decks too much at sea. I am not troubled with great scruples, my friend. But I find that dead men are worse incumbrances than scruples—ashore. They are sure to be found, and when they are found, a howl goes up, a search is made, and even if all comes to no harm, there is nevertheless a chance of delays and a great slaughter of a man's time."

Oliver Perth looked grimly upon him, and then he smiled.

"I begin to perceive," he said "that you are that most rare creature, a man of discretion. I shall be glad to talk with you further."

They pushed ahead more rapidly to his house in the village, where White Harry and the black horse were stabled.

"You are not spreading an alarm?" asked Clovelly in some surprise.

"It would be of no use," the Roundhead replied. "I have been hated so much and so long that I think they would all dance and shout in the street if I were to be shot down in the highway as I came near being, except that their bullet found the life of my poor horse and not me."

He led the way into the house, saying that they could soon talk at leisure, when the foul-faced creature who had opened the door to Clovelly appeared and announced to her master that "Master Bartlett from Bristol" was waiting upon him.

At this Oliver Perth showed the greatest excitement.

"What has brought him here?" he asked furiously. "Does he not know—"

He broke off as sharply as he had begun and strode on into the house, walking unceremoniously in front of Clovelly into a sort of antechamber. There they came upon a brown-faced sailor, big-necked as sailors always are, with a merry grin upon his lips and eyes, thought Clovelly, as hard and as mirthless as those of Oliver Perth himself.

"You?" grunted Perth.

"Me," said the other. "And with news and big news, mate."

Perth hesitated, and then swallowed his anger. He led the

way into an adjoining room, waving to Clovelly that he could see him soon. But Clovelly forgot all about the delay and the disappointment. He wanted no quick interview with Perth now.

He wanted time in which to examine certain facts which had come to his attention and still further to arrange in his mind certain suspicions which had been growing there. The interest in news from Bristol had been as covert a thing as it was intense, and Clovelly was not of a mind to put that interest down as an entirely innocent thing.

In the meantime, he picked up from the floor a bit of a green stick upon which the sailor, Bartlett, had been whittling. All sailors have some skill in manufacturing trinkets with wood and knife, and Bartlett was no exception. He had carved from the soft wood a very good representation of the exterior of a boat during the time he had sat there, waiting for the arrival of Perth.

She was a model of a pinnace, with only a slight sheer fore and aft, a lean, clever-looking boat for smooth waters or rough. He had proceeded so far that he had even indicated her flat bottom and stem post and had begun to carve out one or two portholes along the sides.

Clovelly regarded this crude little model of a boat with an interest so intense that a sweat poured out on his brow. But presently his nostrils caught a faint scent in the air, and this so excited him that he dropped the bit of wood upon the floor, closed his eyes, raised his head, and strove to catch the dim, sweet fragrance again.

But it was gone like a ghost, and finally he was forced to pick up the model again and continue his reading of it.

It was half an hour before the inner door opened and the brown-faced sailor came out with the same jolly smile and the same hard eyes. He seemed highly pleased with his interview with Perth, and as he shook hands he could be heard muttering in a voice which would not be subdued:

"No harm, Mr. Perth. I thought that the figures could be

raised, maybe. And so I come over. No more, because I know it isn't safe. But I just come over to talk about the business. And now I guess we'll both be better satisfied."

With this, he went out, and Perth turned from the door as if he had done a long day's work condensed into his short interview with the sailor.

"Now, sir," he said to Clovelly.

Clovelly climbed slowly to his feet. His mind was in a whirl, for when the big sailor passed, he had distinctly caught the same fragrance at which he had caught before—a delicate and yet a heavy sweetness which followed after him. But who had ever heard of a sailor wearing a perfume?

Clovelly apparently had, and what it meant had thrown him into deep thought. He was now brought into a small study, a grim little room with bare walls which were adorned with only four things, yet each of the four must have cost a considerable sum, for they were oil paintings of eminent Calvinists who had helped the forward progress of the religion, and they had been executed by painters of skill and taste.

The fierce, resolute faces, rather like soldiers than men of God, scowled out of the picture frames, despising the world and particularly all those who looked upon their pictures. This was not the only indication of a religious mind in the room, for upon a table near the desk of Perth there was a great Bible in which were laid a quantity of papers thrusting their edges out from the leaves as if the Puritan had been lately consulting the Old Testament and illustrating some of his doctrines from its pages, grouping together a long list of verses to support an argument.

It was a favorite habit of the Puritans, and it might have made Clovelly smile at another time, but on this occasion it did not fit in with certain preconceptions which were beginning to form in his mind and which made him look almost wistfully at Perth, as though he wished to draw a secret out of the bosom of the latter.

"In the first place," Perth began stiffly, "I find myself under a considerable obligation to you, sir, and—"

Clovelly waved an airy hand.

"Say nothing of it," he declared. "As a matter of fact, the entertainment I had in watching your work against the points of the three rascals more than repaid me for the small labor of drawing a pistol and firing a single shot."

Oliver Perth sighed with relief, as though the effort of rendering thanks had been a strain beyond the telling.

"And now," said he, letting the other matter drop out of his mind, "let us come to the business which has brought you here, my friend."

"By all means—by all means," said Clovelly. "And yet I wonder if my business here is not something akin to the business of the brown-faced sailor who has just left the house?"

Oliver Perth did not start and his glance did not waver, but his eyes widened a significant trifle and then narrowed by as much.

"Ah!" he murmured. "What business, then, do you take his to have been."

"I can only guess, of course," Clovelly evaded. "But—that guess has something to do with a boat, sir."

"It is not hard," said Perth, "to connect that man with a boat. He breathes out an air from the sea at first glance."

"But of a particular boat. I seem to see him in a certain sea and in a certain ship."

"Well? Well?" asked Perth impatiently.

"I appear to see him in a pinnace."

Perth sat suddenly back in his chair and looked more intently than ever at his guest, but he only waved a hand and said nothing.

"I see him," continued Clovelly dreamily, "standing in the stern of a pinnace while twenty lusty fellows ply the oars and the bow wave foams as they work. I see the boat in a warm southern sea, Mr. Perth."

"You are a visionary, I observe," remarked the other.

"And I smell," said Clovelly, "a fragrance—a delicate and strange fragrance such as comes from the dogwood blossoms which are in bloom, say, on the shores of the Bay of Campeachy."

Here Perth lurched to his feet.

"Who and what are you?" he asked sharply.

"A man of discretion," Clovelly replied soberly. "And interested at odd times in logwood, in pinnaces—and in the Spanish Main, sir."

Oliver Perth remained standing and scowling only an instant. Then a grin spread over his features.

He reached behind him, pressed open a secret cupboard, and brought forth from the interior a tall black bottle and a pair of earthen mugs.

CHAPTER XXI

A PIOUS BUCCANEER

"**HERE IS A** brandy," the devout Mr. Perth declared, "which will make you think that the old ship is heeling to the gale again."

And he held the bottle over one of the mugs.

"No, no!" interposed Clovelly. "I have always made it a custom to do my drinking when I was safe in port, but not before I had 'made' the voyage."

His host searched him with a keen scrutiny again, and then, slowly nodding, he clapped the cork into the bottle again and patted it home.

"You have been the captain of one ship at least," he said, "and that the hardest of all to navigate—you are the commander of yourself, Mr. Clovelly."

The latter thanked him.

"You knew Bartlett at once," suggested Perth.

"I did not. I have not seen Port Royal these three years."

"Ah?"

"I have been doing land duty," said Clovelly, and scowled so black, of a sudden, that his host began to nod with more understanding than ever.

"I begin to comprehend," he said, and his sharp eyes fastened on a great white welt which ran round and round the right wrist of Clovelly.

"But," demanded Perth, "what, in a few words, do you want of me?"

"A few words," said Clovelly with equal bluntness, "could never express what it is that I want."

Perth frowned, then shrugged his shoulders.

"I am a busy man," he said.

"I expect in the future," Clovelly asserted, "to make you even busier."

"In what way?"

Clovelly was hard pressed. But he felt that he was coming close to a very exact understanding of this man, and he still feinted and played to make time.

"In the same way," he finally hazarded, "that Bartlett has brought you business."

"Good!" said the other, slowly. "Good! You are in the same work with Bartlett. I had thought that you actually 'made' your voyages with sweat and danger."

There was a suggestion of contempt in this answer and Clovelly hastened to answer: "I did not mean to suggest that I do only what Bartlett does."

"And what, exactly, do you think that Bartlett does?"

"I think that he draws a long bow and sometimes hits the mark," Clovelly ventured, smiling as if he knew much more than he cared to speak outright.

"My friend," said the other darkly, "I have no further time to waste. Either tell me what you will have with me—or pass on your way! I cannot sit here and banter."

"I will have a ship, then," said Clovelly.

"I am to give you a ship? Good! And what are you to give me in exchange?"

"Part of my harvest on certain seas, where the Dew of Heaven falls."

He said this with an emphasis.

"Good!" said the other slowly. "Good! But do you take me for a madman, Mr. Clovelly, and expect me to venture a ship and supplies on your word?"

Clovelly shrugged his shoulders.

"I can show you," he said, "what is worth more than ships and money in Port Royal."

"What is that?"

"Men!"

"True enough. Have you a hundred men in your pocket, then?"

"I cannot talk any longer on this point in this house," said Clovelly.

"Come, Clovelly, the walls are a foot thick on every side of this chamber. Not a whisper can be heard. You could shout at the top of your voice, and no one would be the wiser for it. Besides, why should I spy on you?"

"In my youth, I trusted every man; pardon me if experience has taught me to trust nothing and no one. I must have you outdoors where there is only the wind to listen to what I have to say."

The other stared at him and then shook his head.

"What could interest me and shock the rest of the world so much?"

"Spanish gold, and Spanish blood, then!" exclaimed Clovelly, as though the words were torn from his impatience.

There came a bit of silence, during which they watched each other like two foxes coming nose to nose upon a trail which each felt was his own secret possession.

"You are talking in riddles," said the Puritan at last. "In a word, I do not know you. I cannot be persuaded to leave this house with you, Clovelly, if that is what you want."

The latter looked calmly around him, though his mind was whirling with excitement and doubt. The time had come for him to play his last card, and speak out like one who knew.

"If Bartlett, the damned sneak, with his dried logwood blossoms in his pockets and his smile, doesn't dare to sail the Main, but buys in the loot of others at Port Royal—if he can buy in there and then bring the stuff across to you and still sell so as to make a profit both for him and for you, how much more profit if I were to take my loot straight from the Main to Bristol and meet your agent there?"

Now Oliver Perth was stung, indeed. He clutched the sides of his desk and gritted his teeth.

"Bartlett has been using that huge mouth of his too much," he said grimly.

"I had not a word from Bartlett."

"Then how did you know?"

"It was my business to find out. I could tell you, for instance, what Bartlett brought to you at this meeting, and where you have placed it."

At this Perth gave back as though a sword blade had entered his body; and, schooled with an iron nerve as a hypocrite though he was, he flushed and then grew pale; he pressed a hand over his heart as he fell back a pace and clapped a hand to the hilt of his sword.

"Devils and damnation!" he whispered. "Is this witchcraft or cursed magic?"

"Strange talk," smiled Clovelly, "for a God-fearing man. Strange talk, Mr. Perth."

"Come," said the other. "This is riddling talk. What you know, I care not. I have come to this mind—that I shall not have further dealings with you. If you have gone about me to find out this much, you may go about me again to find out still more, and I desire to be unspied upon."

"You are a man of infinite discretion," Clovelly observed. "Suppose I should bring a hue and cry upon your house. What then?"

"They'd find nothing. A minute after you leave this house there'll be nothing in it that could interest a beggar."

"Not even the hutch, yonder?"

"It will be found filled with holy tracts."

And the rascal grinned broadly, sure of himself.

"But you cannot outface me," he said with a sudden touch of anger. "I have an idea, Mr. Clovelly, that the king's men might be glad to know of you, to hold you and to make a search among your possessions. But in a word I have done with you, sir. Leave me at once!"

He spoke like a king, waving toward the door. But Clovelly shook his head.

"Whatever lies you may have spoken to me," he said at last, "I find that you have told me the truth about one thing at least—which is that you have walls here capable of defying sound. Only those air holes which lead to the roofs, I presume, and then down and out to the open, could convey sound, and I presume that all the shouting you are capable of could not send out noise enough through those small vents to rouse the house."

"Do you talk to me," said the Puritan, "of lies?"

And he secretly drew open a drawer of his table.

"Close the drawer," said Clovelly, and he drew from his bosom, with the languid speed of a moving cat's-paw one of those long and slender pistols. "Close the drawer, Mr. Perth. I wanted to talk to you out of your house, so that we could conduct our little argument in the open, but the longer I think of it the more I see that this room was specially and most happily designed for the very purpose for which I intend to use it."

"Robbery, then," Perth remarked without the slightest indication of surprise or other emotion. "Is that your object? You are a singular fellow, Clovelly. I think I shall have you apprehended before you have fled five miles, but in the meantime here is my purse—"

"Softly! Softly!" cautioned Clovelly. "That was an unhappy movement, Mr. Perth. If your hand had stirred an inch farther, I should now be looking into the face of a dead man."

"It is impossible," said the other with unshaken courage, "that you will commit so cold-blooded a murder."

"My friend," Clovelly declared with a soft voice which made his savagery the more terrible, "I have seen the decks reeking and stinking with blood; I've seen my shipmates go down, gorged with steel in the throat. Do you think that after such sights as these I'd hesitate to blow out the brains of a damned secret knave who crouches here and shows his pious face to the world, while he makes his fortune off the loot which the free-handed buccaneers take on the Main and then sell again for a tithe of its value?

"I admire a good lie, Perth, but I hate a dog who fawns only until he gets close enough to drive in his teeth. In the meantime, use your hands as if they were anchored. Do not stir; you are living within a fraction of an inch from hell."

And he tilted the muzzle of his pistol to indicate his meaning. After that he stepped closer, pushed the gun into the stomach of his host, and then passed his left hand into the bosom of the other. He fumbled for an instant and pulled out a little leather bag of the softest goatskin.

The Puritan groaned as he saw it leave him; he even dared to stir a hand to recover it. But Clovelly now dropped it upon the table in front of his prisoner.

"Open the bag," he said. "Use those two hands of yours to open that bag and to display the contents to me, one by one. I am a curious man, my friend."

There was a stifled curse from Perth, but eventually he obeyed the summons and untied the mouth of the bag. When he tilted it a torrent poured forth, such a cascade as wrung an exclamation even from the guarded lips of Clovelly.

For what he saw first issue from the bag was a little golden crucifix, of which the four points were four brilliant diamonds, and in the crossing was an immense ruby, in itself worth a ship and its cargo. And Oliver Perth groaned again as he saw that jewel exposed.

Next came other objects of a strange nature indeed to be in the possession of so God-fearing a man as Oliver. A half dozen large cut stones, all emeralds and diamonds which had been pried from their settings.

And then there issued forth a brooch of exquisite enamel bearing the arms of Spain—such a pin as a gallant captain of Spain might wear at his throat in honor of his king and his country. Last of all there fluttered forth a slip of paper which Perth crumpled in the palm of his hand.

"And that also," said Clovelly.

"What is a bit of paper when you have these?" muttered his host, sourly.

"It may be the chief jewel of all. Let me see it."

Perth, with another oath, tossed the crumpled ball to him, and Clovelly spread it carefully on the desk. He read:

FRIEND PERTH:
These trinkets are your share as owner of the ship, being one third of the value of the plunder brought home to Port Royal, but in my thinking a closer approach to the half than the third.
BARTLETT.

CHAPTER XXII

THE MEASURE OF A MAN

"**BY THE HEAVENS!**" murmured Clovelly. "It is even as I was beginning to think—the subtle rascal sits peacefully at home and sends out his merchantmen with cannon and powder and shot to sail the Main—and this is his commerce—this is his commerce!"

He folded the paper carefully and placed it in his pocket; he scooped up the jewels and placed them in the same place.

"What a smooth-faced dog of a lying hypocrite you are!" he remarked thoughtfully. "As I suspected, this is the chief jewel of all to me!"

"For what purpose?" asked Perth, his face deadly pale.

"Why, I may choose to let these trinkets and this paper be seen."

"I shall disavow it."

"But Bartlett might be taken and under pressure, my friend, do you think he would be silent? He has a large and a loose mouth, as you yourself have said."

"What devil sent you here?" groaned Perth.

"A woman drew me," said Clovelly with his mirthless smile. "She will be glad to see these things. She will be glad to hear you explain their nature also. You are coming with me now to face young Mistress Cecily Medhurst."

"I'll first be damned!"

"You will walk before me out of your house and into the

street, and I, walking behind, will keep this little toy in my pocket, ready for firing. Do you understand, sir?"

Perth hastily wiped the dripping sweat from his face.

"I see," he said finally, "that you are a man of sense, Clovelly. And now that we understand one another, I think that arrangements may be made to furnish you with that ship you wish for sailing the Main. You hear me?"

"I am already furnished!" smiled Clovelly. "I am already furnished with my ship—" and he tapped the pocket in which that handful of wealth had been dropped.

Perth sank back in his chair.

"To be taken like a fool and a weak coward," he moaned. "My God, to be taken without raising my hand—"

"You are wrong, sir," Clovelly interposed; "I intend to buy those jewels and also the pleasure of your company to Medhurst Park."

"You?"

"You wear a sword, Mr. Perth. I have seen you use it very well. And I, sir, have been hungering for exercise all these dull days. Will you play, sir?"

He arose from his chair, pushing it back into a corner, and dangled his pistol negligently in his fingers. Perth had risen like one enchanted by unexpected good news. He moistened his white lips as he stared.

"Pistols and sword against sword alone?" he asked.

"No."

Clovelly drew forth another gun and placed the pair on the edge of the desk.

"We are now," he said, "equal, man to man—"

"One living—one dead!" gasped the false Puritan and, as he spoke, he whipped out his blade with lightning speed and lunged full at the breast of Clovelly.

No hand on earth could have snatched out a rapier in time to make a parry; but the snaky flexibility of the visitor enabled him to twist to the side, so that the darting point glided through his jacket only and pressed for a cold instant at his side. And as Perth, with convulsed face, leaned in after his lunge, Clovelly staggered him back with a heavy blow of his fist in the face and then leaped away, drawing his own weapon.

They stood opposite each other, their blades leveled, their bodies sharply turned to present the right side only, their left hands poised lightly behind them. And each, as he marked the cold, keen eye and the faultless ease of the other, admitted in his heart of hearts that he had never before confronted a more formidable adversary.

For a moment they hung apart. Then, at the same moment, they attacked. Only lightning skill on the part of each prevented a double death that instant. Their blades clanged, however, and they swerved away from destruction.

Then Oliver Perth attacked in earnest. He fought as one does who has at stake life, or something more than life. There was no fanciful embroidery of mincing steps or wasted handiwork in his style. He darted straight in and out, taking advantage of every inch of his great length of arm and moving with the most astonishing speed of foot.

In a deadly silence he bore forward; the air became brilliant with the dartings of his steel; twice the mysterious speed of Clovelly's gliding feet was all that saved him from destruction, and then he was pressed back into a corner of the room.

"Now, dancer!" snarled Oliver Perth. "The time is here!"

And the long shadow of his body slid across the floor against the feet of Clovelly as the tall man lunged. Yet the sword did not go home. He had prepared the nerves of his wrist for the bitter griding when the point, passing through the slender body of his guest, should bite into the stone wall behind him.

But he barely stopped his weapon before the point was indeed and vainly shattered against the stones. He whirled about with an oath of astonishment and of rage. Clovelly stood smiling before him. Between the drawing back of his hand and the lunge, Clovelly had slid out of the way.

"You are sweating," said Clovelly. "Pause and breathe yourself. This is the most excellent game I have ever enjoyed."

"All the devils in hell!" groaned the big man. "If this is not witchcraft, I am a fool!"

"Then doubtless it must be witchcraft, my friend. But if you will not rest, come again!"

He seemed to hold out both hands, regardless of his sword as he delivered the invitation, and Perth stepped in now with an assault that was truly dangerous. For whereas he had fought cruelly before, he now added utter and desperate recklessness to his sword play; and such a humor makes the most unskilled hand dangerous; it made Perth, for a time, sublime.

The sword was a feather in his hand; it danced in the eyes of Clovelly, or it seemed to become living and supple as it twisted around his guard and bit at wrist or forearm, or snatched at his forward right leg.

Then Clovelly attacked in turn in the very face of that outburst. A time thrust which risked his heart for a chance to split the throat of Perth stopped one of the latter's rushes; another countered the very next attack and brought a gasp from the big man, for the point of Clovelly's weapon had pricked the very ridge of his nose.

He gave back a little, to study the inexplicable adroitness of this assault. And in came Clovelly, still smiling without mirth, as cool and as alert as when the battle began; and Oliver Perth knew that he would die when Clovelly so willed it; he had met his master at last.

"Tell me one thing?" he demanded.

"A thousand, my friend," Clovelly agreed.

"Did old Medhurst bring you here hunting for me?"

"In a manner of speaking, yes!"

"Then—finish and be damned!"

And he literally flung himself at his opponent.

Clovelly leaped back, stopped, swayed in, and his slender blade clashed against the blade of the tall man. The latter felt an upward and sidewise wrench at his weapon and the hilt slid from his wet, sweating fingers.

Far away sailed the rapier in a shining arch and struck against the wall. It landed heavily, rattled against the floor, and Perth leaped sidewise to regain it, expecting the steel in his back as he did so.

But he regained it safely, wheeled with an exclamation of joy that life was still his, and faced Clovelly again. Then he understood. For Clovelly was no longer smiling. He was laughing, and he had lowered the point of his rapier to the floor.

"Come again, Perth," he said. "You have talents as a dancer yourself. They are only revealing themselves."

Oliver Perth, instead, rammed the sword heavily home in its sheath and dropped into a chair. He shook his head at the surprised face of Clovelly.

"What fiend taught you I cannot say," he muttered, "but you are an incomparable master, Clovelly. I had rather die without an effort than show myself a fool. Here is my breast; there is your sword. Finish and be damned!"

"Spoken like a man," said Clovelly, and he put up his own weapon and taking up his pistols, placed them once more in the bosom of his coat. "Spoken like a man, and in fact, my good friend, if you were less filled with—scruples—I should like nothing better than a lieutenant of your qualities to sail the Spanish Main."

His companion smiled sourly.

"If it's not my blood," he said, "what will you have of me now?"

"The pleasure of your company to Medhurst Park."

"You may kill me, Clovelly, but you shall not make me be a witness against myself in front of Cecily!"

Clovelly shrugged his shoulders.

"My dear friend," he said, "you have lost your sense of humor.

You have been living in the very center of a great joke all these years, and now you will not show that you can laugh at a bad turn.

"What is it to you? I do not ask you to tell the rest of the world, but only Cecily, in my presence. The reason is this: she may be a wanton, but it seems that she loves you, and love is a holy thing, Perth.

"Therefore, I intend to see that love killed in her before this hour has run out. She must see the bit of paper, the trinkets, and hear your confession—"

"Not if I still keep my senses!"

"Unless you quite lose them, you will do as I say. What, Perth? You are lost as it stands. I show her this writing and these jewels and you are damned; I am asking you to merely seal your damnation in her eyes by coming with me.

"You lose also, to be sure, your chance of winning the estate by marrying her, and I suppose that that is the loss which pricks you most sharply. But if I do what I can, Perth, you'll not only be in loss of the Medhurst estate—you'll be in loss of your head as well. Your neighbors will come and take you for the crowning hypocrite of the ages and hang you upon the first tall tree!"

CHAPTER XXIII

THOROUGHBRED

"**MR. MICHAEL CLOVELLY** and Mr. Oliver Perth," said the servant, "are waiting upon you, sir." Squire Medhurst came out of his chair roaring like a bull.

"You lie, damn it!" he bellowed at the man. "Perth had rather show his face inside hell-gates than before me. Get out and have the rascal thrown off the place—no—no—I'll come myself to talk with him. I'll come myself!"

He passed from the room with a rush, and presently stormed through another doorway into the presence of Perth and his slender, dark-faced companion. His thick fingers were working, but the squire controlled himself for an instant.

"Gentlemen," he asked, "why are you here?"

"My friend Perth," Clovelly replied, smoothly, "has been persuaded by me to give up certain pretensions which have annoyed you."

"What pretensions?" the squire demanded grimly, still keeping himself in hand, although on the verge of an explosion. "What pretensions? I have seen this fellow only half a dozen times. If I have heard his name more often, it has not been at my desire. What pretensions has Mr. Perth? And to what, Mr. Clovelly, do I owe the happiness of this visit from you?"

"To a letter happily written by you to a gentleman whose name shall be nameless."

The word Ipswich formed on the lips of the startled cavalier, and Clovelly nodded.

"And for what purpose?" asked Medhurst.

"To claim the reward you mentioned."

"It was a hasty letter," Medhurst protested, losing color, "and besides, it required a thing which has not been performed."

"Mr. Perth desires to speak with your daughter," said Clovelly.

"I'll see him burned in hell-fire first!"

"To speak to her in a different tone from that which you expect!"

The cavalier looked at the young Roundhead, and he saw that the face of Oliver Perth, for all of his self command, was spotted and livid with passion suppressed. He regarded this sight for a time with wonder, but then he left the room with Clovelly at his heels. The latter paused and glanced back before he left the room.

"The full truth and only the truth, Perth," he commanded. "I shall be listening."

Then he passed out in the hall where he found the cavalier still in great doubt and staring at his guest with a passion of doubt and of misery.

"Suppose that this is a trap?" he conjectured.

"For what?" asked Clovelly. "A trap to seize on Mistress Medhurst? Certainly two men could not be fools enough to dream of carrying away a woman from Medhurst Park in broad daylight. Or do you think that this is to make an impression upon the mind of your daughter? You have already confessed to his grace that she is in love with the Roundhead."

"The little fool thinks she is. That is all."

"I guarantee, sir, that if she sees Perth he will tell her such truths about himself that she will be cured forever."

"What are they?"

"I have promised to keep them secret."

"Sir, sir, can you expect me to believe that you have persuaded Perth to betray himself to my daughter?"

"Easily. In the first place, there was an affair with our swords; in the second place, I have secured from him certain proofs which speak most eloquently for themselves. He will talk to your daughter rather than have me talk to the rest of the world."

"A woman's love grows on the evilest things that her lover can confess to her."

"Any sin but groveling hypocrisy. Or if this will not do, I shall return to that room and kill Perth before he can leave it."

He stood indifferent, and the squire looked at him as if he were confronting a madman.

"At any rate," said Clovelly, "I intend to marry Cecily Medhurst and start for London with her this day. Otherwise, your honor and your oath are forfeited to his grace of Ipswich."

The cavalier passed a bewildered hand across his forehead.

"What does Ipswich gain from all of this?"

"The pleasure of the game," Clovelly answered. "How will you choose to have this acted out, sir? Shall I go back to Perth?"

And he laid his hand upon the hilt of his sword so calmly that it was not hard for Medhurst to see Oliver Perth already dead in his house. He himself went up to his daughter's room in the old tower and brought her down, without a spoken word, until she was at the door of the room where Perth waited.

She opened the door, uttered a glad cry, and ran straight in to him. Her father closed the door and turned to Clovelly a face withered with pain. He did not speak, however, and neither did Clovelly.

The squire paced up and down the hall. Clovelly sat motionless in a chair, and if his thoughts were busy with that picture of Cecily as she had come down the staircase with her father beside her, he gave no show of it in his face.

There was a brief interval; then Cecily Medhurst burst from the room where she had been talking with Perth, gave them a wild look, and would have fled up the stairs if her father had not stopped her.

Oliver Perth himself came out with a bitter, black face, and stalked down the hall with his left hand resting on the hilt of his sword and the fingers working violently. He paused and turned toward them at the door from the hall, but when he was about to speak, his glance rested upon the horror-stricken face of the girl, and he turned again and strode away with a speed that resembled fright.

"What is it, girl?" her father commanded. "What has he told you? Have you found that your father is not quite a fool, after all? Have you found that I know a man from a man? What did the rascal have to say?"

"Such things, father, that I'm sick—I'm sick to think of them. It turned me cold to hear him talk. I have been a fool; but you will never know how he lied to me before, and what a holy air he had worn. No one could have known him."

The sturdy squire gazed upon her with a mingled joy and sadness; then he raised his head and stared at Clovelly. He sent Cecily not back to her place of confinement, but to her own room; and he confronted his guest.

As soon as they were alone he demanded the full reason why Clovelly had come and the latter told him shortly: word had been given him by his grace that a certain worthy cavalier, in terror lest his daughter should marry a Roundhead whom she loved, had sworn as an alternative to marry her to the first man who should destroy Oliver Perth.

He, Clovelly, had undertaken the task; and he believed that he had been able to succeed in it, although without taking a life. The squire listened to this tale with a heightening color.

"I understand," he said at last. "I have pledged my word rashly: but I had rather lose my life than my honor, and what I have promised I shall act. But, Mr. Clovelly, I think I understand you. It is not the girl that attracts you, it is the thought of the handsome property which goes with her. For the time being, your resources are rather barren. Come, come, my friend, we shall compromise for a round sum of money paid this day into your hand!"

There was no passion in Clovelly's refusal; but his quiet voice was a thousand times more convincing than an explosion of protests. Indeed, his mind was already out of England and sailing the high seas south and west to the Main.

He would go like a conqueror, indeed, for with the ship which Ipswich promised him, and with the spoils which he had taken from Perth to fit it out, he would come in royal condition to the Main to enlist a crew of cutthroats for the work which lay before him.

As for Cecily, she went to his grace to complete the bargain; and if a touch of pity rose in him for her, he had only to recall the scene at the garden gate of the London house, and the words she had spoken to Marberry to disperse his pity quite. It was no sin against her, he told himself; indeed, such a creature as she would be grateful to him because he had brought her to such a master and lover as the famous duke.

It was with these things in his mind that he answered Medhurst, and such was his manner in declining the money bribe that the squire did not hesitate.

"Clovelly," he said, "I see now that I took the long step too hastily. You are a man of iron and will hold me to my word; but I think that I have a right to ask you who and what you are, sir."

"I am a man," was the answer, "named Michael Clovelly. As for what I have been, that is a secret between my God and myself. Is it not a secret, really, with every man, sir?"

"The marriage, then?" said the squire, with a gray face.

"It must take place immediately. Suppose that we allow an hour to persuade Mistress Cecily and to bring the minister?"

"An hour!" cried the poor squire.

"Why, sir, as you know, whole battles have been fought and won in the space of an hour."

The squire departed, and Clovelly remained in his chair looking through the window over the forest and seeing not the tops of trees, but green, rolling waves; yonder low-lying cloud was the sails of a great ship coming over the horizon. He had sent for White Harry, and presently he heard the neigh of the great horse outside the house.

Immediately afterward Cecily was brought into the room with her father on one side and the parson on the other. They made a strange picture, and Clovelly studied them with a detached interest as if they had little or nothing to do with him. The parson was badly frightened, but too much in awe of the squire to hold back from his orders. The squire himself seemed ten years older, although he had thrust out his great, square jaw to signify his determination to go through with the matter.

As for Cecily Medhurst, she reminded Clovelly of a certain man who had faltered and failed on the retreat and had sunk down to await the coming of the Spaniards on the trail. The expression of his face had been like that of Cecily this day.

There were no tears in her eyes; indeed, she had not wept at all, but the terrible bludgeoning of words which she had received showed in the shrinking manner with which she eyed her grim father. The squire now took Clovelly to one side.

"Now, man," he said, "when I offer you money, I'm not speaking of a hundred pounds or so. I'll settle enough on you to keep you as a gentleman for the rest of your days."

Clovelly thanked him without enthusiasm, and declined again.

"But if you go through with this," said the squire, "remember that you are stepping into danger. You will be followed with troubles. And remember, Clovelly, that there is one short way to terminate any marriage. Do not think that it has been out of my mind!"

"Sir," Clovelly remarked, yawning, "I have not the slightest doubt that you will get me murdered if you can. In the meantime, the parson is waiting. I ask one thing as a dower for my wife; and that is a coach for her to ride in, two sound horses to draw it, and a driver."

A furious refusal swelled to the lips of the squire, and was swallowed as another thought came to him. He nodded.

Then he waved to them to proceed, and Clovelly stepped to the side of Cecily and faced the parson. It was a curious tableau.

Yonder sat the squire, with his face bowed into his great hands and the fingers running through his hair, so that it all stood up in a gray forest. Sometimes a great shudder swept through him, as if he realized at that instant that he was casting away flesh of his flesh and blood of his blood into the hands of a stranger. But he did not look up or speak until all was ended.

The young parson, in the meantime, was shocked almost to a nervous collapse by the strain he was under of actually performing the marriage ceremony of the daughter of the squire, of carrying it on under a charge of secrecy which he was to preserve inviolate so long as he lived, and above all his morale was shattered by confronting the flowerlike, frightened face of Cecily and pronouncing over her the words which chained her to this strange fellow "until death did them part."

As for Clovelly, he was watching—quite dissociated in spirit from all that was taking place before him. He was amused by the parson; he rather pitied the squire, but he was most amazed by the actions of Cecily.

Had he not known her to be a lost woman, he would have taken her actions to represent the terror and the grief of the most virtuous of ladies. When he came beside her, she had clung to his arm with a willingness which at first passed a shiver of disgust and contempt through him.

But then he saw by the wavering of her body and by the weight she placed upon him, that she needed that arm vitally to keep her from falling. She stood, in fact, upon the verge of dropping in a swoon; and if the hard heart of Clovelly was not touched, it was at least astonished. And, close to his hand, he felt the tremulous and uncertain flutter of her own heart.

"A strange manner," he communed with himself, "for a

wanton, but no man can understand woman, and he who attempts to do so is no better than lost."

With this thought in his mind he shrugged his shoulders
slightly, and answering the parson himself, he waited for the
voice of the girl, broken with sorrow and tremulous with weakness. But, instead, he felt a stiffening of her body, a tightening
of the small hand which clung to his arm; he saw her head go
up. She paused, drew a little breath, and then answered with a
voice as smooth and as even as Clovelly's own.

He was staggered with surprise, and just at that moment he
caught again a faint, faint scent of the logwood blossoms, more
delicate and far, even, than that which he had dreamed of as
the sailor crossed before him at Oliver Perth's that same day.

He thought it was a mere memory, then, but now it came
surely and sweetly to him. It was no ghost, but by some rare
miracle the girl herself loved the fragrance of those blossoms
and kept them with her for a perfume.

Then, in a wide sweep, half the Spanish Main was unrolled
before him; and the face of the girl was everywhere—her reflec-
tion smiled up to him through the dark green images of the
forest which hung above the clear river—her voice spoke among
the hoarse mutterings of the crew in the forecastle—and down
a forest path before him came who but Cecily Medhurst, with
her hair loosely braided about her shoulders and garlanded with
yellow logwood blossoms.

He shook his head—the parson had been forced to repeat
his next speech twice before Clovelly finally made answer.

CHAPTER XXIV

WIFE

THEY WERE MARRIED.

They stood in the hallway just behind the great door and looked down to the equipage which had been drawn up in waiting for their coming. It was a graceful carriage, made with all the care a jeweler would bestow upon a fine watch—light, built of the finest and the driest woods, seasoned to the toughness of an old yew bow, with strong running-gear which promised to bear the body of the vehicle swiftly and as smoothly as possible even over those terrible roads of the seventeenth century.

Clovelly bestowed upon it the fine eye of appreciation with which he would have looked over a pirate ship, and after all the use of this carriage was to be equally dangerous, although in a lesser way. With a pirate ship he sailed the broad seas in the face of many enemies, each large enough and strong enough in men and guns to blow him out of the water if it came within gunshot, and so with this dainty carriage he was to thread the forests and the highways in the face of many enemies by land, fully as fierce and as resolute and far stronger in proportion, than his enemies by sea.

For the hand of the king—which meant ten thousand hands—was raised against him; and there was the power of Oliver Perth, utterly unscrupulous and as cunningly used as a fox and as savagely applied as a wolf; and there was the squire himself who had already made a surly promise to break this marriage with death, and who was apt to ride on many a long mile and with many a hardy follower before he would confess that his daughter had been safely stolen away from him by a single unknown man.

Nor was this all, for there was the other balked lover—young Pennistone—whom he had tested and knew to be a man. Pennistone would surely fly to arms and to horse and, with just half a word from the girl's father to encourage him, would plunge away with a score of men to undo the deed which the parson had accomplished on that day.

He was called from his reverie by the voice of the squire at his shoulder.

"Mr. Clovelly, here is Nelly Curtis, who has taken care of my girl for twenty years, very near. I suppose that you'll want to take Nelly along with you?"

"Ah?" murmured Clovelly, and he turned and viewed a broad-faced, honest-eyed woman of forty with a smile ugly enough to have broken the heart of a strong man and kind enough to have healed it again. She now supplied her best curtsy with all her best grace to gain the first step into the favor of her new employer, but Clovelly appeared to fail to see her.

"For the present," he said, "one woman is enough in my cargo."

Nelly Curtis gave back a step with a wan face, and with startled eyes that looked first to her mistress and then desperately to her old master for help. The squire called Clovelly back.

"Are you going to stick at this?" he questioned, softly but savagely.

"I'll be the captain on my own deck, and with my own wife," Clovelly replied, dryly.

"You damned fox-face!" moaned the squire. "I'll have your hide off your bones for that! There aren't enough roads in England to keep me from you, Clovelly. Write what I say in red!"

He turned gloomily to the others, where Nelly was standing

in a strange way before her mistress, as if she would protect her with her last act of service from the brutality of this stranger who had stooped like a hawk to sweep her away—and beyond Nelly was the pale face of Cecily.

How great were her eyes and blue as the deep blue sea; and how golden her hair—like the slant rays of a tropical sun! But she held herself as easy and as dignified as if she were a queen facing those of whom she was the undoubted mistress.

"There's no use, Nelly," said the master. "He wants no servant with him. But maybe he'll change his mind, and Cecily will be back here with us after all—after all!"

There was no mistaking his meaning. It whipped a fierce color into the face of Nelly, and she eyed Clovelly as if he were a snake. In the meantime, two stalwart fellows were bringing down a heavy, iron-bound box.

"Is that," asked Clovelly, "for the carriage?"

He was answered that it was.

"Put it down, then," he ordered. "I like enough cargo for ballast, and no more. I'll never take that hulk inside my boat.

"Madame," he continued to his wife, "open the box and take from it what you most need—and only that. And I promise you that you will not need much."

"I have no care," said Cecily patiently. "It matters nothing."

"By all the gods!" thundered the squire. "Are you a man or a cruel devil, Clovelly?"

"You," said the buccaneer, heedless of the others and pointing to Nelly, "open that box and take out of it what your former mistress will most need. Quickly, because every minute I delay ties a pound of lead to my heels."

She hesitated, looking sulkily to the squire.

"Quickly," Clovelly exclaimed, with a cold ring in his voice, and the woman jumped as if he had lashed her.

She tumbled the box open and, as if guided by instinct, whipped together the necessaries. Clovelly from the tail of his eye saw a fluff of silks, then some heavy dark clothes, a strong coat, a bonnet, and a pair of serviceable boots. He nodded with content as she made the bundle ready; then he turned to the nearest servant.

"Bring me paper and a pen," he directed, and when it was brought he scribbled a few lines and shoved it into the hands of the squire. The squire read:

> I, Michael Clovelly, do hereby renounce all claims upon all moneys which have been entailed to my wife, Cecily, from the estate of her father, and freely render back to Mr. Medhurst all of our claims in the property.
>
> MICHAEL CLOVELLY.

The squire, reading this amazing document, felt his raging blood curdle in his veins; for wild tempered as he was, there had never been a passion in his life which could not have been controlled for the sake of such a sum as was here signed away.

Clovelly, in the meantime, had taken the arm of his wife and led her down to the carriage. He put her into it with the aid of his driver.

"No delay," said he. "But I greatly fear that we be already late. No whipping, my man, but a good stiff rein on those nags for the first five miles and don't stop for the bumps."

The driver gave him a keen look, as if surprised and gratified at one and the same time to find that his temporary master has sufficient knowledge of horses to give such directions for the journey. Then he clambered onto his seat and loosed the reins.

Poor Cecily was snatched away in the midst of her farewells by the forward lurch of the coach, and they whirled down the winding driveway with the final cries of love and of farewell rising to the pitch of a wail behind them.

They passed the great outer gate; they rumbled over a mile of road; then Clovelly bade the coach turn sharply to the side down a narrow lane. He himself led the way, for he had mounted on the great, strong horse, the gray stallion, White Harry. In a secluded spot of the woodland he raised his hand and when the coach stopped he motioned the driver to dismount; he himself did the same.

"Follow me," he said to the man, and to his wife—how strange was that word, even when it came silently into his mind—"Whatever you see or hear while I am away, do not leave this carriage. Do you hear me?" he added as she remained silent.

"I hear you, sir," the girl replied.

He stalked away with the driver until they were fifty paces from the carriage; then he whipped his two pistols from his bosom and fired twice. The first shot cut in twain the twig on which a rook was perched. The second shot killed the heavy-winged bird as it arose with a clamor. And he turned now to the driver, who was watching him with a scowl, one big hand thrust into a pocket and there plainly clutching a pistol in his own defense.

"What is your name?" asked Clovelly.

"Dunbar," said the fellow, making no effort to raise his voice from a growl of hatred and suspicion.

"Dunbar," said Clovelly, "I have done this to show you that I am a man of a suspicious nature and that when I see anything calculated to make my suspicions seem well founded, I never hesitate to fire—and when I fire, I kill. But when I am well served, I give from the bottom of my purse. I see that you wear a ruby, Dunbar."

The fellow glanced down, still scowling, taking a pace back so that, while he glanced at the ring on his thick brown finger, he might not be surprised by Clovelly.

"I do," he admitted.

"What is its value?"

"It's a true pigeon-blood," Dunbar replied. "Why do you ask?"

"I see," said Clovelly, "that you know rubies; you've studied them, eh?"

"I was given this by my old master, Squire Deans," said the

fellow. "That's why I know about rubies. I could sell it for—enough! But I keep it for the old squire's sake. Why do you ask?"

"If you know rubies, then." Clovelly remarked, casually, "you'll be able to appreciate this."

He felt in his pocket and presently brought out that great central ruby which had stood fixed in the center of the cross which he took from Perth. It blazed like a live coal in his palm.

"Take this, Dunbar," he said.

And to himself he added: "There I throw away the price of a ship of a hundred tons, of the most exquisite and solid construction; and I throw away the cost of the guns to furnish her, and the price of her rigging—all of this to secure the good faith and the services of one half-baked rascal whose master has told him to betray me when the opportunity offers."

Thus he communed to himself, in the meantime studying carefully the face of Dunbar, which was now a curious mask in greed, fear and above all an overpowering astonishment. But Clovelly continued to talk smoothly while the grimy fingers closed and unclosed over the great stone.

"It is a great treasure, Dunbar, is it not? But you possess a greater treasure of which I am now in need, and that is honest service and good faith. I have shown you how I can reward a traitor"—here he touched his bosom, where he had replaced the pistols—"and I now show you how I shall reward an honest man. The squire has told you to give me lip service, and to be ready to trip up my heels—but if you served the squire for a hundred years would you earn the cost of such a stone as that?"

Dunbar pressed it between both of his hands. Then he lowered it gently into his pocket as if he dreaded lest it might burn its way through the lining and so escape from him.

"Yes," continued Clovelly, driving home the bolt which might hold the man to him, "those who work faithfully in my service grow rich. Think not to judge me, Dunbar, by the coat I wear.

I tell you that I have made men rich; for I know that fearless and faithful service is worth treasure."

There was no doubt about the effect of these words on Dunbar. He had considered the speaker at first with a wild and roving glance as though he were hearing a tiger speak with a human voice, but now a great light dawned upon him.

"Sir," he said, "they've lied to me about ye; that's what they've done. They've lied to me about ye!"

"They have, Dunbar, and from this time on, whatever strange things I do, act like a man of sense and believe that I have another meaning than may appear."

Dunbar nodded and touched his hat; and at the same time the fingers of one hand clutched at the pocket which contained the ruby.

"I can't hit twigs, sir," he told Clovelly, as he drew out an immense horse pistol, "but I can hit a man as far as this old gun will throw a bullet."

CHAPTER XXV

AMBUSH

THEY FOUND CECILY sitting erect in the carriage, perfectly still, with only the tightness with which her fingers were interlaced to tell of the terror that she was in; for perhaps to her that sound of shooting had meant murder. The patterning of the shadows of the branches fell softly over her, and Clovelly eyed her beauty with a sort of sad disinterest.

If she were his, unstained, what a prize she would be to keep against all the world, to serve like a queen, until she made for him a heaven upon earth. But since she was as she was, she was no more than the dirt upon which tall White Harry strode.

The carriage started on again. It was drawn by two grays, and they scampered along at a round rate with the carriage swaying and rocking and groaning. Then Clovelly rode past the coach and took the lead as they swung down a hill and pointed for a road in a hollow which was heavily covered with a row of trees on either side.

"There may be as many men in that gulley," called Clovelly to the driver, "as there are teeth in a wolf's mouth; but look where the road forks. I am going to ride straight ahead; if a fire breaks out at me, I shall try to ride the gantlet, but do you swing aside to the other road and I shall try to join you, if I escape, by riding across country."

Dunbar waved his hand. He made a queer, squatty figure of a man on the driver's seat, his booted feet braced far apart, his narrow head sunk deep between his shoulders, and his great hands fixed upon the reins. On either side of him, fastened with loops of leather to the seat, were the huge horse pistols, and slung in a leather case over the side of the seat there was a huge-muzzled, short-barreled blunderbuss, which cast a handful of lead and broken iron at a discharge and might sweep a whole width of a road clean of enemies. So prepared, he waved his hand to his captain and then sent the grays gingerly down the hill, using his brakes to keep the carriage from running down too heavily upon them.

Clovelly, in the meantime, roved on ahead, gathering White Harry beneath him for an emergency. What a horse it was! It seemed to read the mind of its master, signaled down the taut reins and to the iron bit between its teeth, and now White Harry became a bundle of half coiled watch springs waiting for a word or a touch of the heel to loosen them all together.

He danced into the heart of the hollow and Clovelly, glancing back, had barely time to note that the carriage had not yet come to the forking of the roads when there was a considerable rustling on either side of the road and two tall men rode out from shelter with pistol leveled not at him, but at White Harry. All that they wished to do was to dismount him, counting upon other means to handle the rider.

Those other means were not hard to guess, for there was still a whispering among the shrubs on each side of the road, and the keen eye of Clovelly caught the glinting of sharp bits of light upon gun barrels here and there. They had come out in force, indeed, to stop him.

He dropped the reins into the crook of his left elbow and so was able to put up both his hands. At the same time he checked White Harry to a slow trot, but all the while the stallion could be controlled by the pressure of knees and heels rather than of the reins.

"You have me, gentlemen," said Clovelly, his hands high above his head. And then, as he came closer, he saw that it was the least dangerous of all his enemies who had been able to set such a trap for him. It was young Theale, Lord Pennistone, who had brought these men together and blocked his way.

There might be thirty men in the ambush. It had been cunningly planned, too, keeping them all in the background, saving two leaders, who, when they blocked the road, gave the signal which caused the others to close in from the sides.

At the same time, he saw Pennistone and his companion elevate the aims of their pistols to his own breast. He was completely helpless, but with the reins dangling from one elbow and with the supple little whip hanging from his other wrist, he came on toward them, his hands hopelessly high.

For that position was his only way of disarming them and their attention for even an instant. Lord Pennistone began to give orders like a soldier, and indeed, he had served abroad and under the ablest captains.

"Herbert and Matthew!" he called, "bring out half a dozen and close the road behind him, Joe, block the road ahead. The rest of you lie fast and take your aim at him. We must make sure that he doesn't break through the bag now that we have him in it—"

"Hello!" called some one, "the carriage has taken the other road."

And indeed, faithful Dunbar had swung the coach to the left-hand fork of the road and now the wheels were making a distant thundering behind the trees.

"Let that fool driver go!" cried Pennistone. "We want the fox, and here we have him. Never mind the rest. They'll be bagged in due time. Clovelly, halt your horse."

"Very good, sir," said Clovelly, checking White Harry to a slower trot and then to a fast walk, as if he intended to stop the stallion just before them. "I find myself hopelessly outnumbered, and there is no shame, I believe, in surrendering to a greatly superior enemy?"

"In France it is so considered," Pennistone agreed, bowing.

"I regret that I must ask you for your pistols and your sword, sir."

"You are entirely welcome," Clovelly declared, but instead of reaching for his sword, to bring it out for surrender, being now full upon them, he twisted his hand suddenly so that his fingers caught the handle of the whip and slashed it across the faces of both of his antagonists, for they were sitting their horses side by side.

It was a cutting blow, and as accurately aimed as any sword slash, for it bit them over the eyes and half blinded them. They fired off their pistols with a roar of oaths and of pain, but they had fired blindly.

As for Clovelly, he dug his heels into the tender flanks of White Harry and the big gray shot away like a thunderbolt. He crashed between the two mounts which stood before them. His powerful shoulder cast one to the ground, horse and man.

Lord Pennistone's horse was flung far to the side, and White Harry was instantly among the honest fellows who, at his lordship's command, had just filed across the road to block his advance. But not one of them had his weapon in a position to fire. An instant before yonder was their man calmly surrendering to their master, and now he was crashing through them on a horse which looked as huge and as winged as a thunder cloud.

The three or four immediately in front of him fled for their lives from the giant animal; the others turned about, pitched their guns up, and fired a scattering volley. They found an elusive target, however, which was already a vital distance away, for Clovelly had swung his mount under the shadows of the line of trees on his right.

That dappling of shadows which fell upon him and White Harry made them a more difficult target to strike. He was flattened in the saddle, and even so one slug slashed his coat at the shoulder and another caught his hat and knocked it clean from his head.

He twitched White Harry through a gap in the trees, and at the same instant the whole body of men down the road belched a volley after them. The bullets rattled among the branches and brought down a shower of leaves around him, but that was all.

He rode ahead, unhurt, and turning in his exultation he shook his fist behind him, then went on, bringing White Harry down to a moderate gallop at once, so perfect was his surety that he would escape.

He now swung the stallion back into the road. Those behind him had fired their volley; but by the time they reloaded he would be safely beyond them and the only danger in which he lay was from their pistols; yet how could pistols strike at two hundred yards? Yonder came half a dozen riders, however, spurring their horses, with sword in one hand and pistol in the other.

He only laughed at these, and called gaily to White Harry. The big stallion took wings over the hill; he jumped him over a tall hedge on the farther side; leaped a broad creek in the middle of the field; cleared a wall on the farther side, and finally found himself upon the other fork of the road, with the pursuit fallen to a dull and drowsy sound of shouting in his rear.

One thing he knew—they would not jump those fences but would wait until they found the gates in them; and comforted by this thought, he brought White Harry back to a conservative pace once more and went on again, blessing the giant strength and heart of that good mount.

He came upon the carriage almost at once. Dunbar drew up his horses to a slow trot and as he drew alongside, the girl stood up in the carriage and stared at him like one reclaimed from the dead.

"Thank God!" he heard her cry more to herself than to him. "There is no murder done."

He pondered that voice and those words for a moment, but he had no time to waste upon her and her emotions. Instead, he communed with Dunbar at once upon the goal for which they should strike that night. He could get nothing but exclamations from the coachman at first.

"When they poured around you, sir," he said, "and when they held their pistols to your head, and when I saw that your two hands were over your head, I'd a mind that you'd never look me in the face again, nor your wife neither. And then I heard the guns roaring. 'He's tried to get away,' says I to myself, 'and they're blowing him to bits with their blunderbusses!' But I went on down the road. 'His ghost 'll haunt me,' says I, 'if I pull up and wait to see what's happened!'"

Having expressed all of this astonishment, which Clovelly allowed to go unanswered, the master now inquired about the inns toward which they could aim, and he found that Dunbar was a treasure indeed, for he knew the country, every inch of it, as if he had once made a map of it. He could rattle off places and distances as fast as he could talk, never pausing to guess.

What Clovelly decided on was a rash thing, indeed. He had the coach turn to the side, again, at the first lane they encountered and so they came back to the main road to London and Clovelly straightened the coach out upon that highway once more. He announced to Dunbar that they would drive straight down that highway and stop only at dark for the tavern.

The pursuit, he explained, probably would comb the side roads; they would never suspect that a man like himself might dare to use the main highway. And at the tavern there was only one chance in four that some one would recognize Cecily Medhurst, or the carriage in which they were traveling.

Dunbar gaped at him at first, then nodded curtly, as if he now understood why that ruby had been given him; he was to fight for it and his master and the lady, and from the manner in which Dunbar thrust out his chin it was plain that be did not intend to be slack in his duty.

CHAPTER XXVI

MASQUERADE

"**HARKEN TO ME,** madame," said Clovelly to his wife as they drew near to the tavern that night. "Hearken to me—you are no longer Mrs. Clovelly—you are Lady Dunstall, being on your way to London with your husband's secretary for your service. You may call me Michael. I shall expect you to carry your part, madame."

She nodded and bowed to him and then sat back as she had done all the afternoon, with a pale face and with troubled eyes looking to the far horizon. He bit his lips at that, foreseeing only lame acting on her part, but when they reached the inn she carried it off with a manner that astonished him.

Clovelly went in to engage the rooms, but when "Lady Dunstall" entered and inspected her chamber, she found that it would not do at all, and made a great complaint and insisted upon seeing half the other chambers in the building before she would be content. As for Clovelly and Dunbar, they were forced to sleep in the attic along with the other servants.

Dunbar accepted the company of his master with a quiet pleasure, and during the course of the evening he attempted twice to draw out Clovelly in talk, but it was like talking to a stone. Just before the falling of the utter dark, Clovelly went down to the room of Cecily and tapped at the door.

She opened it to him at once and he found her with her bright hair sweeping in a glorious curve over her shoulder. She gathered her dressing robe closer about her bosom and shrank

back from him in a fear as terrible as it was silent, but Clovelly hardly looked at her.

"I forgot to tell you," he said, "that you will sleep in your
clothes and be ready to leave at any time in the middle of the
night."

She swallowed; she was still too paralyzed with the fear of
him to speak.

"Can you get to the ground through that window?" he asked
her.

She motioned him to come in and see for himself; so he went
in and closed the door behind him, and stepped to the window.
It would be simple indeed to leave in that fashion. An infant
could have climbed down the slanting surface, using the crev-
ices in the stonework as steps.

"This will keep you," he told her gravely. "My signal to you
is this:—"

He clapped his hands together, and followed with two quick
blows. "Whether it is a stamp upon the floor, followed by two
quick stamps, or a whistle heard in the same measure, you will
be ready to leap out of your bed and to go through that window."

She nodded.

"Good night," said Clovelly. "And I wish to thank Lady
Dunstall for playing her part so well."

"But tell me, in thanks," she pleaded suddenly, "why you have
taken me, where you are leading me, what you will do with me?"

"Why do men marry?" asked Clovelly, frowning.

"Because they love the person or the estate of some girl, or
because they are tired of living alone, or because they are in an
adventurous humor; or for a dozen other such light reasons."

"Well?" Clovelly inquired. "Do I not fit into one of those
categories?"

"I have seen scorn in your eyes," she said. "I am nothing to
you. I saw you resign your claim to a great estate through me.
You want neither me nor my fortune. What is it, then, that you
wish to do with me?"

"A thing, madame, for which you will thank me much."

"A thing for which you have to-day risked your life as if life to you were a cheap thing that could be worn out and replaced at the first shop."

"That for which I am playing is worth gambling with death."

"What is it, then?"

He shrugged his shoulders.

"In the name of God, sir," she begged, with a tenderness of sorrow and fear coming into her throat again, "have compassion on me. I am haunted with a terrible anxiety all the day. I shall not sleep tonight."

"The stake for which I am playing," he said, with that mirthless and slow-dawning smile, "concerns the lives of a thousand men, I hope; it concerns the lives of whole towns, whether they shall stand or burn; it concerns such things, madame, that your blood would run cold, I hope, if you heard them all. But it is something I can never reveal to you. Only I swear to you that what I am to do for you will, in my estimation and in my reading of you, make you think yourself the happiest woman on earth."

"In your reading of me!" she cried. "But is your reading right? My own father has believed a lie about me; he has read me wrong. How can you tell that you, sir, have not read me wrong? And I entreat you in the name of mercy, let me know to what I am traveling."

He had started, and his dark face grew black, indeed, but now he shook his head.

"I cannot be mistaken," he declared. Suddenly he added: "I wish to ask you, madame, where you learned to care for the scent of the logwood blossoms?"

As he spoke, he drew a stick of the blood-red wood from his pocket.

"The blossoms?" she echoed him. "But how do you even know what they are? I have never before found a man who knew, excepting one. Have you been there, Mr. Clovelly? Have you been on the shores of Campeachy Bay?"

He would not answer her, but as he hung in the doorway, uncertain whether to go or to stay, it might have seemed to Cecily Clovelly that she had indeed shaken this strange fellow.

"Good night," he said at last, and left her.

As for Cecily, she dropped into a chair and sat for a long time with her chin in her palm, watching the fire, until some of her terror passed, and eventually, as though she remembered something, she began to smile. But Clovelly went out from the interview and stamped into the night.

A rattling rain had blown up, but he hardly knew that the drops were falling, stinging his face and his hands and drenching his clothes; for his mind was rioting wildly. He could not take a dozen paces together without stopping for thought, and every time he stopped he ground his knuckles against his face.

"If there was ever," communed Clovelly with his dark soul; "—if there was ever one who spoke with the voice, and looked with the eyes, and stood with the courage of the pure of heart, it is she. And if she is pure, I am damned utterly and terribly if I bring her to the dissolute Ipswich."

This surmise made him halt again, groaning; but he would say to himself: "No. These round-eyed girls with their bright hair and their sweet smiling could cover up the black designs of the devil himself in their secret hearts."

And, with this comfort, he would stamp on again. It was late before he turned back. Then, coming to himself, he discovered that he was tramping almost to the ankle in mud across an open field, with only the pitch dark and the slanting rain around him.

It cost him an hour of exhausting labor to find his way back. He had to guess the direction by remembering how the wind had been blowing that evening when it began to roll up the clouds of this storm in the sky. Then, by the slant of the rain, he guessed at the points of the compass and started to explore for the inn.

When he came to it, it was so late that he had to tap at the door and get mine host up, who grumbled and growled about "drunken fools serving great ladies" until he unbarred the door and saw Clovelly go past him, streaming mud and water as he stepped. Mine host was then too astonished to protest against the staining of his floor and he gasped as Clovelly went up the stairs.

Clovelly was recalled from his reveries by the boring of the eyes behind him. When he whirled about suddenly and looked clown, he saw the dismayed and suspicions face of the host.

"I have played the devil with my secrecy," he said gloomily to himself as he went on toward the attic. "If there is the least chance of exposing us, mine host will do his best. He trusts me now as he would trust a tiger; he probably thinks that I have been out doing a murder."

There was nothing for him to do, however. So he went straight on to the attic, took off his clothes, wrung the water out of them hard, and then put them on again, rolled himself in a blanket and in spite of his drenched skin went instantly to sleep with a faint, dreamlike recrudescence of the delicate savor of log wood blossoms in his nostrils.

CHAPTER XXVII

MINX!

IT WAS A thread of sound as sharp as the edge of a Damascus blade; it not only awakened Michael Clovelly, but it brought him at once into a sitting posture and then upon his feet. His head rang and sang with it. But just what it had been he could not tell, for it had struck him, so to speak, in the very heart of his sleep, and he could not carry his understanding of it into his waking moment.

The smoking light was still burning in the room, but now, as he looked about him, he saw that Dunbar was not in his place where he had been when he himself returned from the midnight walk. The wet clothes of that walk were growing icy cold upon his back and now a draft which stirred through the room made him shudder. It, at least, cleared his mind a trifle and he said to himself: "The rat has left me; he guessed that the ship was sinking."

The instant he had muttered that to himself he was sharply aware that there was no one in the attic chamber to overhear him. He stared about him again. The ragged blankets lay here and there where the wretched grooms had lain in sleep. But they themselves were gone; there was not a man in the place, of all those who had been there earlier in the night.

Now he was wide awake. These movements of his mind had taken the space of a second or two only, but as full consciousness dawned upon him he knew the thing that had roused him from

170

his sleep—it had been a scream. In the night a woman had shrieked as if in mortal terror or in an agony.

At that, he was through the door and the rapier flashed into his hand. There was a chance, and it seemed a large one to Clovelly, that the cry had come from the lips of the girl he had married. When he thought of that, he forgot all the disgust with which he had looked upon her before, remembering only her clear eyes, her beauty, and the sad sweetness of the fragrance of the logwood blossoms.

He leaped down the narrow stairway to the first turning. As he swung around it, he heard a whisper like the hiss of a blade coming from its sheath. At his very feet he saw two bulky shadows crouched upon the stairs with the dull glimmer of steel in their hands and Clovelly, leaping back, swung his sword in a sharp circle before him.

His speed of foot could not have saved him here, but that "universal parry," as the rascally Italian fencing master and street brawler had called it, stood him in stead. His slender weapon clashed against two, flung their points aside, and gave him the tenth part of a second to decide whether he should try to break through them or retreat.

They did their best to help him come to a decision. The two were not alone. Others were looming in the shadows behind them.

"Cut for his legs, Charlie," growled one voice. "I'll put my point through the throat of the dog."

And they lunged at him in unison. There was no time for circular parries now, no matter how universal might be their nature. Clovelly, like a man of sense, turned on his heels and fled for his life. He gained the attic room again in time to slam the door and shoot home the bolt which guarded it.

But that frail security promised to hold only the briefest moment. The thrust of one heavy shoulder would break the door in. He added another bolt of a differing nature by shouting:

"I'll pistol the first rascal to come in!"

"Bear back, mates!" roared a thick voice. "The main thing is to keep him here while the other work goes on. Steady, lads. We'll have the fox out of the hole when we're ready to take him. There's time enough on our side,"

Clovelly was already at the window, but, hearing this, he had half a mind to go back, open the door, and strive to rush down the stairs while they were taken by surprise, but he was no reckless madman. He controlled that impulse at once.

Whatever might be the "other work" which was going on—and he needed small wits to guess that it had to do with Cecily—he could not help by attempting to storm a fortress. Instead, he looked down to the ground through the window, and he had no sooner taken the survey than he acted to take advantage of it.

He swung himself through at the very moment that a new-comer up the stairs hurled forward at the door and brought it down with a crash. Clovelly climbed like a cat to the ground and crouched there an instant.

Voices were bawling in the room which he had just left. The whole hotel was wakened; here a woman screamed; there a man was shouting for a light; another was cursing at the top of his lungs; heavy feet crashed against the floors; lights swung in the windows.

But Michael Clovelly felt that his grand adventure was completely lost. The girl was gone from him, and he would never be able to retake her. And, writhing and grinding his teeth, he cursed himself as a fool for ever pausing to take shelter in a hotel. He should have made straight on until the horses died—then still ahead with others until they came to the lights of London and victory.

A door was being battered in the lower part of the building. He followed a blind hope and raced around the hotel to the window of the girl. Luck was good to him here. It was against her very door that they were still pounding.

It was too lucky to seem real. But, after all, it might be that they had presented themselves at that door only a few seconds before. They had gone there at the same instant that the men went up the stairs to reach him.

He was at the window in a trice. Past the edge of the curtain he saw Cecily cowering in a corner of the room, dressed completely. The batterings ceased for the instant. For the door was of the stoutest oak, secured with two thicknesses laid in opposite directions. It had defied the assailants so far, although they had sadly shattered and broken it.

"Cecily! Cecily!" bawled the angry voice of her father. "What the devil, you stupid minx? Will you undo the bolts?"

"Father," cried the girl, her voice trembling with fear, "I cannot manage them—there is some trick—I cannot tell—"

"You lie, you little fool!" thundered the irate squire. "You've grown enamored of the cutthroat who has taken you off. But I'll have you back from him. I've sealed my bargain by letting the knave take you; now let him keep you if he can. Lads, have down the door. Damn the host. I'll manage his business for him later on."

The last no doubt implied that the landlord had attempted some mild remonstrance for having his house broken into, his guests roused from peaceful sleep, and his doors battered down. Clovelly had not the slightest doubt that the squire, with a few weighty gold coins, could make all right and well. Medhurst was too rich to be treated like a common law-breaker.

At the same instant a guarded voice panted close beside him:

"Mr. Clovelly—in God's name—off with you! I've hunted the place up and down—"

It was Dunbar. He gasped out that he had had only a short sleep that night, awakened smelling trouble, and had gone out to saddle the horses and have them ready in case of an emergency. He had heard the disturbance—now the horses waited at the edge of the wood. He had "borrowed" a third saddle. There would be no driving in the light coach that night.

"Go back to the horses," said Clovelly, when their location had been pointed out to him, "and stand by. I am coming with the girl, or not at all."

There was a startled: "Aye, aye, sir!" from out the darkness, and then Dunbar was gone. Clovelly instantly threw up the window while the battered door sagged at the center under the impact of the next blow. It cracked from top to bottom and plainly could not hold out against many more strokes.

He was ready to enter the room and carry her away by force, but there was no need. At sight of him, she held up her hands in a mute thanksgiving and ran to the window. One frightened glance she cast toward the door; then she was outside and at his shoulder.

"Much as she loathes me and dreads me," thought Clovelly to himself, "she dreads and loathes her father still more."

He helped her to the ground; at the same instant, four men turned the corner of the building at the run.

He heard the girl's moan of terror, felt her sink against him in the weakness of dismay, but he had no time to do more than close his hand strongly upon her shoulder before the four were around them.

"Who's this?" called one, and another took Clovelly by the shoulder and turned him toward the light which streamed down from the window.

Clovelly struck the rude hand away.

"What ails you, fool?" he shouted. "The rat hasn't come this way. Have you had a sight of him yet? Is that why you're so hot on a trail?"

The other replied with an oath.

"I thought our fortunes were made a second ago," he grunted. "And here's nothing but some of the hotel's party. But head on, friends. We may round him in later. Keep your eyes sharp. Remember that the man to seize him will never have to work again. The squire has sworn it."

They dashed away, and Clovelly felt the girl straighten beside him once more.

"Brave, by the Lord!" he said as much to himself as to her. "If you had let them see you wince an inch, they would have had us! Cecily, you should have been a soldier!"

As he spoke, he was hurrying her across the field toward the place where he could already make out the glimmer of huge White Harry. But not he alone, it appeared, had been able to distinguish the outline of the giant stallion. The door to Cecily's chamber had gone down at last.

There was a thundering shout of rage and dismay when the empty chamber was discovered, and now the window was filled with the head and shoulders of the squire himself, crying:

"Look alive on the outside! The bird has flown! The bird has flown! All the devils have come out of hell to help her! A hundred pounds cash to the first who sees them—a hundred pounds cash—!"

It was a fortune, and the thought of a fortune will make men see through the very darkness itself. Some one made out the gray horse at the edge of the trees, and, of course, that color was known as the horse which Clovelly had ridden.

A shout went up to tell of the discovery, like the opening bay of the hounds when they first cry on the trail, one loud cry to give the signal, and then a score of voices chiming in to take up the trail.

"Run!" Clovelly pleaded to the girl. But she had already taken to her heels and raced across the field as if she had been winged.

CHAPTER XXVIII

UNSEEING

WHEN THEY REACHED the horses, Dunbar was there, ready for his work, and he tossed Cecily into the saddle. Clovelly saw her dexterously gather the reins as the horse reared and plunged away. She clung like a cat, and was instantly in command of the excited brute.

Dunbar, however, had no such easy task. His mount had caught the contagion of excitement and began to dance with a head thrown high and foolish panic in its eyes. Dunbar dangled at the end of the reins, making ineffectual efforts to master the head of the horse.

So much Clovelly saw as he whipped onto the back of White Harry. And doubled was his strength when his knees pressed against the smoothly muscled sides of the charger, and when all that thunderbolt of courage and power and weight and speed was gathered in the hollow of his left hand where the reins joined.

The men had far outstripped the rest of the pursuers, sprinting desperately in the hope of attaining that rich reward which the squire had promised to the lucky man who first laid hands on Clovelly. They were closing fast, one with a sort of cutlass flourished in his fist and the other poising an old broadsword which had seen service in the armor-hewing contests of an earlier war.

The challenge of Clovelly checked them. Then, in a leap, White Harry was upon them. Imposing at all times, when he

176

plunged forward with the wind lifting his silvery mane, and his ears flattened along a snaky head, the great animal appeared half demoniacal. The two stalwarts aimed feeble blows at the thin air, and then fled for their lives.

But it was not the purpose of Clovelly to pursue. Three strides of White Harry would take him among the main body of the squire's hired bullies.

Clovelly veered the charger about and found Dunbar even then settling himself in the saddle and, with one foot in the stirrup and the other iron flying wildly in the air, galloping full speed to the assistance of his master.

Such dogged loyalty touched even so grim a nature as Clovelly's to the heart. Yonder was the girl, too, flying among the trees. Once he lost sight of her, he might as well strive to find a ghost on this dark night, for though the moon was high in the heavens, the wind was hurling black cloud-masses into its face and it looked down on them only with short, wild glances; it gave only enough light to show the picture of the wild storm which was making riot through the upper air, while mere vagrant breezes skirmished across the ground.

So he cried: "Follow me, Dunbar! Let the others go and be damned to 'em. Ride for your life, man!"

With that, and a mere loosening of the reins of White Harry, he was off—truly like a white arrow from the bow. Before the disappointed men of the squire could level their pieces, he was out of sight, and they fired their random shots at Dunbar, who pursued hotly the form of his leader.

Even all that speed could not bring Clovelly up with the girl. She had twisted away among the trees, and he lost her; he had to shorten rein and raise his head to listen before he heard the crashing of her horse through the underbrush.

Again he glimpsed her, as White Harry stormed forward like a creature possessed, literally beating his way among the saplings as if they were stalks of brittle grass; but again the girl disappeared among the thousand alleys of the woodland. He drew rein again, breathing hard and cursing his fortune, but a rattling which he heard was the first of a brisk shower which, with a fresh gust of wind, soon filled the forest with noise.

The last guide which he could follow to her was lost to him. Here was faithful Dunbar shouting behind him, hopelessly lost. He called, and the stout fellow spurred instantly to his side.

"Is all well?" he cried.

"Be silent!" answered Clovelly, full of grief and malice.

Then, with a ringing oath, as he saw his protracted efforts fail and the stirring vision of that tall ship sailing for the Spanish Main vanished from his eyes, he touched White Harry with the spurs and galloped away blindly through the wood, careless of what he should find. But how miserable a failure was this— to have baffled so many attempts of strong men, and then to be given the slip by a girl—by a mere child!

The rain roared in a sudden torrent about him. He raised his naked face to the downpour, heedless of what boughs might loom to knock him from his seat, only feeling in the sting of the rain a fierce pleasure.

The rain stopped as quickly as it had begun. There was only the dripping of the water from the soaked leaves, and the rushing of White Harry and of Dunbar's horse well in the rear. They came out into a road, splashing through a puddle that dashed him with muddy water to the knees. He drew rein again, and as he stopped, above the panting of the horse he heard, in the thin distance, the wailing cry of a woman: "Michael! Michael! Oh, Michael!"

It was a thunderbolt of amazement to Clovelly, for why should she be calling, and above all, in his name? Would the prisoner call for the jailer when once the sweet air of freedom had filled his nostrils?

But an explanation came hastily to him: The horse, plunging through the wood, had brushed her from her seat. And now she lay bruised and sick, half buried in the wet mud, broken in spirit, and crying for help.

He was off in the direction of that cry before the explanation had taken full form in his mind. He shouted. The answer came tingling back to him, far richer to his ear than the cry of "Sail, ho!" on the Spanish Main. For she was that prize to redeem which Ipswich would pay the value of a tall ship and a tight ship, and a crew of hardy ruffians such as he yearned to lead.

So he broke out into an opening and there—ah, double wonder!—she was sitting quietly on her horse, which was per-fectly under her command, and above her head a great branch projecting gave her shelter. It was not need which had made her cry out his name, and had she willed it she might have taken her way whithersoever she chose, and above all to the arms of that infamous old dandy in London, Marberry.

For she had not flown. The bird had seen the cage opened and yet had fluttered back to imprisonment, of its own free will.

Compunction came rarely upon Michael Clovelly, but it smote him now as he reined White Harry so sharply that the great stallion leaned back on his haunches and came to a stop throwing up a great spray of water and mud before him. There was something, then, which Clovelly did not understand, but this was only the beginning, for a greater wonder lay in wait for him.

She rode out to him from the shadow of the tree and so into the white down-pouring of moonshine as the wind scoured the clouds away from the heart of the sky for that instant. She came with that light in her face, and a smile of welcome.

She came holding forth one hand to him, and as she drew near he heard her breathe: "Oh, for a moment, Michael, I thought the firing of those guns meant—but that was a horror, and here you are, come to me!"

The heart of the pirate rose in him. The high ship, and the ranged cannon, and the dark-faced men, and the heaving deep-blue ocean were all blotted from his mind, for they were as nothing compared with her loveliness.

But the heart of the pirate died again in his bosom. For she had been the light-of-love of another man, and all that beauty was tainted, and all the radiant charm of that smile was fool's gold, and no better. So his face grew stern as he looked down on her, saying:

"You were free, Cecily. You were free from your father and you were free from me. Why did you stay?"

All the joy went out from her eyes. He thought at first that she would break into a storm of protestation, but although the words trembled in her throat they were not uttered. She only bowed her head and murmured brokenly:

"You will never understand—you will never trust me, Michael!"

"Never!" he answered savagely. "God be my help that I may never lose the wits of a man because a girl simpers at him! I tell you this frankly, Cecily, in order that you may know me. If you can go free of me once again, do so in the devil's name, and never come within the reach of my hand. If you can leave me once more as you have left me to-night, ride, ride till your horse falls dead, and then run on foot to put miles between us. I tell you this, in order that the game may be even between us."

He added slowly: "And yet, why should I tell you this? For the thing to which I take you, you will consider a paradise!"

He struck his hands together and broke into a loud laughter that had no cheerful ring of mirth in it.

"Where will you take me, Michael?" she asked him.

"A short road to heaven on earth—for you!"

"Heaven on earth for a bad woman—that is how I read your words!"

"Good and bad are things to be juggled with—not to be understood, No more of this."

"Only this much—that I shall never, never try to escape from you. And if others were to take me away from you, I should try with all my might to come back."

He raised his hand.

"Do you think that you have here before you," he demanded,

"some callow boy who has never heard the wiles and the oiled tongue of a woman before?"

"And yet, Michael, suppose that you should be wrong? Suppose that you should be wrong about me?"

"Can the eyes of a man lie—can his ears lie?" he cried at her, enraged by such brazen outfacing of the horrible truth.

"Only once in ten thousand times. Only once!"

Deep masses of cloud washed across the moon again, and deeper darkness rolled across the mind of Clovelly. She had put into words the very doubt which had leaped into his brain the evening before. If he were wrong—

He looked about him. Save for him and the girl, the clearing was empty. Dunbar had ridden out of sight. And that angered him. Did the tactless fool think that he, Clovelly, would waste time and thought on sentimental speeches to another man's mistress?

But still that thought rang in his mind like a bell: What if he were wrong?

He rode close to her, and, leaning from the height of White Harry, he passed one arm about her and with the other hand he pressed back her face until he saw the glistening of her eyes just beneath his own.

"Say it, girl," he commanded fiercely, "as you hope for heaven, say it if you can after me: 'I am free from spot and stain, body and soul!'"

There was a little pause; the water dripped steadily from the trees; the frogs droned in a chorus from a near-by pond.

Then she said:

"I am free from spot and stain, body and soul!"

"You lie from the bottom of your heart!" he cried brutally. "Tell me again in another way: Have you never loved a man?"

There was quiet again, and the beating of his heart shook both their bodies, and he breathed the sweetness of her rain-wet hair.

At last she sighed: "Oh, Michael, Michael Clovelly!"

"Is that an answer?" he cried in rage.

She did not speak, and, releasing her, he reined back the stallion.

"Ride on at my side!" he commanded her curtly. "Dunbar!"

Dunbar rode out before him, and so, all three, they turned again into the open road—but, alas, how the heart of Michael Clovelly was aching!

CHAPTER XXIX

A VENAL RAPIER

HIS GRACE OF Ipswich had thrown off his waistcoat. He had jerked from his neck a collar of the most precious lace and opened his shirt at the throat for easier breathing. And now with his hands clasped behind him, walking up and down the room, or standing in an inspired attitude, or pausing at a table upon which stood two bottles of old Medoc with the chilly, damp cobwebs still clinging about them, and from which he poured a glass from time to time, the nobleman dictated line by line to Randal, who sat in a corner, quietly attentive, scratching down the words with a hasty quill the instant they were uttered.

"What will you say of her, Randal?" asked the master, coming to a halt in his pacings.

"Your grace, it is far from me to—"

"No hypocrisy, rascal! You have opinions. Every man has where a woman is the subject. Your lame beggar who knows nothing more than the price of oranges feels free and able to pass an opinion about a queen; for the worst of those who go in trousers feel, in some devilish fashion, that they are able to speak down to the best that dress in skirts. Am I right?"

"I have no doubt that some—"

"Nonsense! I say, you have seen her. I'll have your opinion!"

"I should say, then, that the lady is generally considered extraordinarily proud, your lordship."

"Proud she is. It is grained in her to the bone. Proud, then, and witty?"

"I have not heard it."

"And you will not. Is she lovely, Randal?"

"She is—unusual, your grace."

"Unusually odd in face and figure. There is the sum of the vixen, then—a proud termagant, stupid, ugly, and distinguished only for her loose manners and her self-esteem. Then answer me a riddle."

"To the best of my ability."

"Tell me, admirable Randal, why I am dolt enough to waste this evening composing a poem which the fool cannot understand when I deliver it to her hands?"

"I have only the ability to guess, sir!"

"Guess, then, and be damned!"

"It is because another person, of the greatest distinction, has chosen to honor the lady with his attentions—"

"Randal, you are profound. That is it. It is because Old Rowley has chosen to waste time on this creature that I see something in her. Any deer is worth a man's marking when it lives in the king's park. Am I right?"

"Most unquestionably, sir."

"Then my time is not wasted."

"May I dare to suggest—"

"Out with it! What will you say?"

"That your time may be worse than wasted. His majesty has a hard way with those who venture to poach upon his own—"

"A hard way with any but me. But I bear a charmed life with him. A charmed life, Randal, because I fought and starved and went through beggary for his sake in the old days—but in the meantime, where is Lascelle?"

"I have sent for him, sir. I have put upon him your express command, and he has vowed to come to you this day."

"It is already nearly night. Does the dog dare to put me off?"

"That is not possible, sir."

"Tell me, Randal—for you have made the fullest inquiry about him—is this Lascelle indeed such a mighty blade?"

"He is considered matchless."

"So I have heard—so I have heard! Would God I were five years younger and in exercise—I should test the sharpness of that matchless point. But perhaps he dares not show his face since he killed poor young Godfrey."

"I believe that there is no fear of harm coming to him on account of that; at least, not from the crown's officers. Old Godfrey, the squire, came and fell on his knees and begged the king for justice."

"Did he do so?"

"This morning. And the king vowed to him that Lascelle should not escape from the kingdom alive."

"What!"

"But after Godfrey went off, his majesty explained to some about him that it would be a pity that so able a swordsman should ever leave the realm, though there was no reason why he should die in it until age took him off—or a better fencer. The rumor has it that Old Rowley intends to use Lascelle in some of his own affairs. He has rivals to chastise."

The last words were said with a certain meaning which made the duke frown.

"Do you intend me by that phrase, you rogue?" he said to Randal. "Well, though I am far from my best practice, I shall not turn my back on any blade in the world.

"But to continue with Lascelle's qualities: if he be not of the finest mettle, I fear for him at the hands of Clovelly. That piratical scoundrel is a fighter of parts."

Randal waved the suggestion away. "I have the entire history of Lascelle," he replied. "The truth is that he is the man who killed Darnac in Orleans two years ago."

"Is it possible?"

"It is the very truth!"

"Then he is matchless. I saw Darnac fight young François Grise, and at that time I considered Darnac peerless with the cold steel. But it was Lascelle who killed him? I thought it was a street brawl and that numbers did for poor Darnac!"

"I have the whole story from the lips of one who saw the fight. It was in the street, to be sure, but it was fairly contested. Lascelle killed his man after he had himself been run through the left arm."

"Good! Skill and a touch of the lion heart, also. That is what we need to mate Clovelly."

"I only wonder that your grace should have designs—"

"Against Clovelly?"

"May I be pardoned for wondering?"

"You may. In short, by all the gossip that flies about the town, Clovelly has escaped ten thousand dangers and is fast approaching, bringing me the lady according to the contract. But I begin to regret that contract, Randal. The lady is lovely, but the price is high. A ship fitted from bow to stern and manned with choice cutthroats—that is a great deal for one amour. If Clovelly has won her by the sword, it is only fair that he should lose her by the sword, is it not?"

"Assuredly."

"But now to return to madame. Since she is a proud vixen, I must address her as a gentle and lovely saint. Begin again and tear up and burn what you have already written. If she is proud, I shall be humble."

He began to dictate:

"Lady, since bitter darkness was poured down
Upon me by your silence and your frown,
My heart is lost in shadows manifold,
My heart is lost and lonely and a-cold.
Cruel and sweet, look forth on all that's living:
Those only are content who most are giving.

"There's a line that is not bad, eh?"

"An excellent line, sir. Worthy of John Dryden himself."

"A fig for John Dryden! He is a fashion, not a poet. But to continue:

> "Consider, God enriched us with His treasures
> Not to be hoarded but to spend in pleasures.
> Oh, lovely miser, what a wealth has lain
> Untouched in you, who only spend disdain!
> But if you scorn my person and estate,
> Yours is the touch of gold to make me great;
> For only the simple magic of a smile
> Shall so transform—"

A knock sounded at the door.

"Whoever it is," said his grace, "be it Rowley himself, send him about his business. The muse! The muse! I feel the muse upon me. Now every second is turning to diamonds of beauty. Alas that they should be wasted upon the person of a fool! Go to the door, Randal."

Randal, accordingly, went to the door. But when he saw who stood without, he made no attempt to execute the order of his master, but instantly stood back, setting the door wide ajar.

"Your grace," he said, "M. Lascelle is here!"

A tall, big-boned man, whose sunken cheeks and deep-set eyes were given a yet fiercer appearance by the narrow trim of his beard and by his long, well trained mustache, stepped into the doorway, and, sweeping his cloak about him, made a profound bow to Ipswich.

The latter forgot his poem in a trice. He started from his chair with a smile of pleasure.

"You are Lascelle!" he said. "So? So? You are Lascelle?"

"I am he, your grace," said the hired swordsman.

The duke waved him into the room, signaled Randal to leave and close the door, and then drew himself up to his full height, facing the Frenchman, while his glance went over the bravo from head to foot.

"The peerless Lascelle!" muttered Ipswich again. "Peerless? Well, well—let it pass! I see you wear the new rapier—the bodkin pattern which lets out a life with a needle prick."

"It is true, your grace," said the other, speaking in perfect English but very slowly. "And there is no sword, permit me, except this. The others are clubs, axes. They hack and beat out the life; this little tool of mine makes the meeting with death as short and as sweet as the kissing of lovers' lips."

"H-m-m!" murmured Ipswich. "Well, Lascelle, I am about to give you a commission which, if you execute it, will make you rich in my favor, burden your purse with a hundred pieces of gold, and give you so great a name that you can coin your reputation into a thousand pounds a year."

Lascelle bowed again.

"In short, Lascelle, you are to encounter, in my behalf, a man about whom half of London is at this instant buzzing. I mean, Clovelly!"

There was no doubt that that name had reached the ears of Lascelle before this moment; instinctively, his long, powerful fingers touched the hilt of his sword. Then he bowed again.

"I know of M. Clovelly," he said significantly. "Did your grace say a hundred pounds?"

"For such an encounter? Certainly not! Two hundred, Lascelle!" Ipswich explained smoothly.

"It is enough," said the other judicially.

"Good! Randal will tell you the details of the plan and lead you to the place. But here it is for you, in short: While all London knows that this madman, Clovelly, is driving on toward the city and making his way in spite of the devil himself, no one can quite guess his goal. But I know it. It is a certain small house on the edge of the town, where there is more country than city and the smell of the fields in the air. To that place

Clovelly comes, and the lady with him. And there, Lascelle, you must go to encounter him with your sword."

"And the lady?" asked the villain, lifting his brows.

"She is not to be touched. As for her, she will be provided for in different fashion. You understand, Lascelle?"

"I do," growled the Frenchman.

"Another thing," said his grace, catching at a new idea. "If you meet him fairly and squarely, sword to sword, I shall add another hundred pounds. For I wish to be hidden near by to enjoy the battle. If what I hear of you is the truth, it should be worth that price!"

"It will be short—but priceless," said Lascelle, with a smile of satisfaction.

His grace frowned.

"Beware of confidence! And remember that while your mere reputation may kill men for you in France, in England you will find different metal. Be sure of that! Drink no wine from this day. Take enough exercise to be sure of your wind. I swear, Lascelle, that you will need all your wits and every scruple of the length of your arm!"

"I shall kill him," said Lascelle slowly and sneeringly, "by bits. He shall die five times instead of once, for the pleasure of your grace."

CHAPTER XXX

THE MURDERER'S ART

THE LITTLE VILLA of his grace of Ipswich lay on the Oxford Road on the edge of the town. It was no pretentious place for so great or so rich an owner. It was hardly more than a cottage settled well back in a wild tangle of trees and shrubbery through which a winding carriage road approached its door.

And along that road three riders slowly rode their horses on this evening. The sun was already down and the last color had faded from the sky, but still a pale band circled the horizon and the twilight was stronger than the radiance of the moon which hung well above the tops of the eastern trees.

In front rode Cecily and Dunbar, weary riders upon weary mounts. In the rear White Harry and his master were as alert and untired as when the long ride began. The great stallion danced upon a loose rein, restrained rather by the voice than the hand of the master, turning his head here and there to look among the tangles of the undergrowth, stopping once with a snort to look up as an owl drifted low above them and across the white face of the moon.

They came before the black front of the house. There Cecily Hampton reined back to the side of her legal husband.

"This is the place, Michael," she said with a sort of sad foreknowledge. "But what will you do with me here?"

"God knows, Cecily," he answered. "Wait here with Dunbar."

He rode around the corner of the low building. Now he saw

one light burning dimly behind a single window. The back of White Harry raised him to a level with the casement and, looking in, he saw an old woman sleeping in a chair, her head twisted sidewise with weariness and the relaxation of slumber. But, even in her sleeping face, there seemed to Clovelly to be more bitter malevolence than in any waking countenance he had ever seen before.

He tapped at the pane. Instantly she started up. There was no fear in her at this summons. She went straight to the window and raised it.

"Who's there?" she asked.

"Open the door to us," said Clovelly. "Go to the front of the house and open the door to us. I bring a guest for your master."

The crone yawned, leaning into the darkness so that she might see him more closely.

"You're Clovelly," she nodded. "You're Clovelly!"

And she began to laugh in a shrill, broken voice that made the blood curdle even in the veins of that captain of the Spanish Main.

"Old witch," said he, "you need the whip! Open the door, and at once."

She hesitated, as if a burning retort were upon the tip of her tongue; but, changing her mind, she closed the window and disappeared.

Clovelly went around to the front of the house again, and presently the door was opened.

Through it he led Cecily, with Dunbar close behind them. They came into a little reception room, warmly and delicately furnished. A hanging lamp was lighted.

Then Cecily, as if all at once she understood, took his arm and clung to him. Her breast was touching his hand, and he felt the hurried beating of her heart.

He knew her face was white and raised to him, but he dared not look down, for he had turned sick in his soul. He saw Dunbar, scowling with doubt, facing him on the farther side of the room. What other eyes might be peering at them from the doorways which emptied into thickest gloom on either side of the room?

"Cover your face!" he commanded.

And she, without a word, lowered the hood of the riding cloak which she was wearing. It did not cover all her face; it merely placed it in shadow out of which great eyes burned steadfastly at Michael.

He felt himself growing weak. There was such an atmosphere in this house that he could not breathe. Yet it was not over-warm, and he wondered at himself. He dashed open a window, drank in a long breath of the chill night air which instantly rolled in against his face, and turned to the hag again. Her eyes had not left the face of Cecily, prying and glittering at her with a pitiless speculation.

"Is there no one here to meet me?" asked Clovelly.

"In the court! In the court!" chuckled the crone. "There is some one to meet you in the court, sir."

Clovelly stared at her. He had grown half suspicious, and yet he knew that sometimes extreme old age made people gibber like fools or madmen. He could not but attribute the sinister ways of this hag to the same cause, and yet he thought it as well to investigate.

"Dunbar," he said, "go into the court and find who has come there to wait for me, and why the devil they wait in the court—"

He turned to the hag.

"Conduct this man," he said, "and have a care that there are no tricks. I come from a country where old witches are hung up by the thumbs. D'you hear?"

She shrank from him, but still sneering, and so took Dunbar from the room. The interval Clovelly spent in pacing to and fro, turning hastily at the end of each beat back and forth that he might not be forced to face the girl.

She had grown more terrible than a regiment of soldiers to him, and yet she was doing no more than following him with her eyes, back and forth, back and forth through the room. He strove with all his might not to see her, but he could not help but notice, now and again, the glistening of her eyes and the pale glimmer of the hands which were folded in her lap.

Why did not Dunbar return? For every instant with this suspense continued was putting the greater weight upon him.

Once he paused just before her and cried: "Cecily—"

She half raised from her chair. There was a broken and a panting tenderness in her voice.

"Yes?" said she eagerly. "Yes, Michael?"

Instead of continuing, he turned sharply about and resumed his pacing. But he was trembling from head to foot; there was such a hunger in his arms to take her body in his arms; there was such a hunger in his heart to be possessed of her soul; there was such a mad, sweet knowledge in his blood that if he so much as stopped frowning she would weep with delight—that all of these things stopped his breath and made hie heart riot.

Yet, Dunbar did not return.

He stamped his feet and shouted:

"Hallo! Hallo! Who's there? Dunbar!"

The long echoes boomed softly through the house, whispered, died and whispered again, but the honest roar of Dunbar did not reply. Only the crone came again to the doorway.

"Old she-devil," said Clovelly, "where is my man? What have you done with him?"

"I took him to the court, fair my master."

"What kept him there?"

"The wine, I doubt not. There is good drinking there—"

"I'll be at the bottom of this foolery. If you are right, Dunbar shall sweat for this. Come, Cecily!"

The crone led the way. He cautioned the girl as they went on:

"Stay close behind me. If there is danger, press close."

Then the old woman opened a door and bowed them through.

Clovelly found himself looking into a sort of Spanish patio—
more of a garden that a court, and with a stretch of smoothly
shaven turf in the center of the plot. There were a half dozen
strong lights hanging under the eaves, and these made a bright
illumination. He saw no men at first, but as he stepped through
the doorway he was seized upon either side. It was useless to
struggle. Upon each hand one man held his arm, and farther
back stood assistants with leveled weapons. A tall man with a
pointed beard and long mustache was approaching across the
court.

"Hold fast, my friends!" he commanded. "Take the girl—"

Clovelly struggled so suddenly and desperately that he half
freed himself.

"Touch the lady," he said, "and I'll find a way of cutting your
hearts out!"

"Let her be, then," the tall man ordered. "She shall look on,
for this will be worth observing."

He came before the captive.

"You, sir," he said, "are that famous man, Michael Clovelly?"

"I may be Michael Clovelly," said the latter, "though not 'that
famous man.' And you, whatever you may be, must know that
the owner of this house is no common man. You will wish that
you had entered hell sooner than invaded his property."

The other waved his hand, so lightly dismissing such thoughts
of unpleasantness to come.

"I may be known to you," he suggested proudly. "I am Pierre
Lascelle!"

"Lascelle? Lascelle?" muttered Clovelly. "I have heard that
name. Ah—Darnac—by my life, it is the same! One Pierre
Lascelle was he who killed the great Darnac in Orleans."

Lascelle bowed.

"Then, sir," cried Clovelly, "I have the pleasure to tell you that
from one who saw it I have learned that you won with a foul
stroke!"

Lascelle stiffened.

"A lie, monsieur!" he said.

"Tush!" Clovelly sneered. "You say that to one whose hands are held."

"They may be at liberty sooner than you wish," the other remarked darkly.

"Call off your bloodhounds," said Clovelly, "and give me freedom to answer."

"It shall be done," Lascelle agreed in his slow voice, in the meantime running his eye up and down the body of Clovelly as if he were choosing in what place he might kill his man. "It shall be done. But, *monsieur,* you are newly alighted from a weary journey. I would not have any advantage on my side. Will you first rest?"

"Bravo!" said a distant voice.

"By heavens!" murmured Clovelly. "I am brought here to make a show for spectators. Who spoke there? I know that voice! Who spoke there?"

"One who will see your body interred properly and decently," Lascelle replied. "Have no fear of that! Come, *monsieur!*"

He turned his back, and walked out to the center of the turf. There he removed his coat, tucked up the sleeves of his shirt, cast off his hat, tied back his long, flowing hair with a ribbon, and, drawing his sword, tried its flexible strength and the agility of his arm with two or three passes into the bodiless air.

By his instructions, in the meantime, Clovelly had been released, and he hurriedly made the same preparations, then stood forth, sword in hand.

"Here," said Clovelly coolly, "are four men of yours. Yonder I see poor Dunbar bound hand and foot and even gagged. Suppose, Lascelle, that I should win—what would my victory obtain for me?"

"Suppose that you should win?" echoed Lascelle incredulously. "By Heaven, *monsieur,* do you hope for that? Well, in case you win, no hand will be laid on you. You depart?"

"What assurance have I of that?"

"A better than mine!"

"Yes!" affirmed the same distant voice which had spoken before.

Clovelly turned toward the point from which he had heard it proceed and bowed low.

"Most excellent and invisible spirit," he said, "I thank you from the heart. M. Lascelle, begin."

"First," Lascelle demanded, "upon what particular quarrel?"

"First," Clovelly replied, "because you have given me the lie. Is it enough?"

"Enough! Begin, *monsieur!*"

"Second, I accuse you here, formally, of killing my master, Darnac, with a foul stroke."

"Ten thousand devils!" groaned Lascelle in fury. "Begin! Begin! It is more than enough!"

"After you, Lascelle!"

The latter did not wait for a second bidding, but instantly leaped to the attack with a long lunge full at the throat of Clovelly. The stroke was parried. They circled each other with dainty, mincing steps, light as thistledown in the autumn wind. Now one darted in, the swords tangled with a light, fierce chattering of slender steel against slender steel. Then they leaped back with the blades still humming from the force of the parries. And the narrow weapons seemed a length of shivering light from the many strong lamps which were burning under the eaves. Three times and again they closed, but still there was no result.

Clovelly set his teeth. He had lived his life with the feeling that the greatest master of all had been Darnac. Now a cold doubt entered his mind. Perhaps this long, grim-faced murderer was a still greater man with a rapier.

For his own part, the long ride had made his knees weak, his feet heavy. The chill of the night air was not yet out of his muscles. And he knew that a desperate struggle lay before him.

CHAPTER XXXI

UNDYING MALICE

WHILE HE MASTERED himself, and as the blood began to circulate more quickly and his limbs grew supple, he fought for time strictly on the defense. But before three exchanges, Lascelle seemed to realize the strategy of his antagonist, and he flung himself heart and soul into the combat.

It was a masterful attack. The blade alone, deft as it was in the hand of Clovelly, could never have saved him from those assaults, but in his own peculiar fashion he danced back, swerving his body from side to side before the assault.

Once the darting point leaped so close that it touched his temple near the eye; again it slipped through his shirt and rubbed its cold length against his naked side.

For five minutes, death was constantly before him, but at the end of that time the numbness had left his legs, his wrist was again flexible, and he had regained that perfect balance upon his feet which is of all things most necessary to the fencer who fights for his life.

He had been driven to the edge of a plot of roses before that time of self-mastery came to him. One backward step would entangle him hopelessly in the soft mold, and to gain that advantage Lascelle pressed his attack with a relentless fury.

The smiling confidence with which he had begun the battle had left him. His expression was a settled and malignant sneer. In every thrust he fought to kill with the hunger of one ac-

customed to slaughter. Sweat glistened upon his forehead from his work, but his eyes were brighter than ever.

The crisis had come. In the distance, Clovelly saw the four men crouched in the intensity of their interest, following the attack and the defense with little movements of their hands, as though they recognized the working of two masters here and were intent not to miss one portion of the lesson.

There was the crone, too, laughing in the moonshine and the lamplight, and rubbing her withered hands in a savage ecstasy.

There, last of all, was Cecily, with her hands clasped, and her face raised. She was praying—and for his victory!

"God in heaven!" cried Clovelly to his heart of hearts. "If she is not true, there is no truth on earth."

He put by thrust and lunge. He gave back an inch in spite of himself, and felt his right heel sink a little in the treacherous, soft garden earth.

"More art, *monsieur!* More art and less strength!" he said to Lascelle. "I have played with you long enough. In a moment I begin to give you a lesson."

"You dog!" snarled Lascelle. "Here is the final stroke!"

And he lunged to the full of his long arm and agile body. But venom had made him hold that stroke an instant too long, and beating it aside with a strong parry, Clovelly side-stepped into the open, and danced away from the garden edge into the center of the turf where the footing was firm beneath him.

There was a general shout to attest this important achievement, and again the voice of the hidden watcher:

"Bravo, Clovelly! Lascelle, you are matched!"

Lascelle repaid that exclamation with a snarl, and closed again. A feint, a lunge, a thrust in rapid succession. Then he rushed in past the point of Clovelly until their bodies struck together.

There was no room to use swords then. There was no time to shorten the weapons, either, and Lascelle, twisting his leg about that of Clovelly, cast him off balance and threw him heavily.

It would have been the death of any ordinary man, but Clovelly was no inert and stunned figure. He landed on the turf as a cat might have landed, and twisted lightly to his feet again.

Even so he would have died, but Lascelle, thrusting murderously when his man fell, had missed his twisting target and passed half the length of his rapier into the turf. Before he could disengage his point, Clovelly was on his feet.

"Foul!" cried the voice of the hidden watcher. "A foul stroke, Lascelle, by Heaven!"

"The fortunes of war!" answered Lascelle, panting with his work. "Luck has saved you, Clovelly, for the last time."

"Hear me, Lascelle," said Clovelly, anger making him cold, according to his peculiar nature. "This is not Clovelly. It is the ghost of Darnac come to take revenge upon you. I remember now. It was such a trick as this that killed Darnac. But it has failed now. You are a dead man, Lascelle."

"You lie!" groaned Lascelle.

But he gave back a little, as if to recover breath, and looked furiously around him at the black faces of the four men who watched, and who had instinctively run closer at this display of unfair tactics.

"Aye," said Clovelly instantly, "look around you, Lascelle.

Your last look at the moon. Your last scent of the night wind. You have not a minute before you. Darnac—Darnac—is waiting!"

And he leaped in to the attack.

Lascelle gave back, returned with a counter assault, maintained even war for half a heart-breaking minute, and then retreated again.

There was a tumult in the court. The hidden watcher was shouting his enthusiasm. The four men, quite won over from Lascelle by his recent exhibition of foul play, now cheered the victorious progress of Clovelly. But the latter fought even more with his tongue than with his sword.

"Stand fast, Lascelle," he panted. "Brave Frenchman, do not run away, I beg you!"

Lascelle grinned in the savagery of his hatred, but he dared not waste breath upon an answer. Still the dancing point of the Englishman's rapier was before his eyes, and still he retired.

"Beware the soft ground!" cried Clovelly suddenly.

Lascelle, in spite of himself, uttered an exclamation of fear and leaped to the side—straight into the point of Clovelly's weapon! A swerve at the last instant saved him from a death stroke, but the leaping steel pierced his left forearm between the elbow and the wrist and brought out a quick flow of blood.

A fresh shout came from the watchers. And now a richly dressed man ran into view. It was that hidden watcher with the vaguely familiar voice. It was the Duke of Ipswich.

"His grace," said Clovelly, "has come to see you die. Now, Lascelle," he added ironically, "for the glory of France. And remembering that narrow, dark street in Orleans where you murdered Darnac—"

"Devil!" groaned Lascelle, and drove in for the finish.

He came half blindly. The narrow sword of Clovelly danced, then the flicker of the steel went out, and the point was deep in the Frenchman's body.

He fell without a groan. The rapier, still clutched in his hand, was drawn across his breast.

"Clovelly," he gasped. "I am a dead man."

"I hope not," said Clovelly. "I hope not, Lascelle. A villain I have no doubt you have proved yourself this night; but I pray that death will not rob the world of so fine a fencer! Come here—in the name of God, some one with a skill in wounds, come to look to poor Lascelle—"

The four came running. Ipswich himself was hurrying forward when Lascelle muttered:

"It is too late, my friend. I feel the darkness in my brain. I felt the sting of death when your point entered me. Well, I have given it to enough! I have given it to enough! Lean closer to me, *monsieur.* I have done a foul thing to-night in this battle. I shall repay you with a confession."

"Of one thing only, Lascelle. Confess to me that when you destroyed Darnac in Orleans it was not through fair battle—"

"Lean closer—lean closer! I am weak, Clovelly. I have no strength to speak loudly."

Clovelly, holding back the others as they ran up with a gesture, leaned above the dying man.

"Monsieur," said Lascelle, "all who say that they saw me kill Darnac lie. The street was empty. What happened was this: I had fallen by tripping on a damned loosened stone. As Darnac stood above me, I cried out for mercy. He accepted my surrender like a gallant and generous man, and as he leaned to lift me from the ground, I stabbed him thus!"

He had been moving his sword as he spoke, until the point was addressed to his target. Now he thrust suddenly at Clovelly's breast. The latter was no better than a dead man, for no movement of his own could have saved him from the sudden and treacherous thrust, but one of Lascelle's own companions, who had been watching his face intently, jerked Clovelly sharply to the side, so that the point of the fallen man's sword pricked through his shirt only.

"A thousand curses!" groaned Lascelle. "You, De Graumont, I shall return from the grave to haunt you!"

De Graumont shrugged his shoulders.

"I saw the devil come into his eyes," he said quietly, "and I knew by that that there was trouble coming. God be thanked that I acted in time or this murderer would have taken another victim with him to hell."

"Lascelle," said Ipswich, speaking with a voice full of horror and yet with something of compassion as well, "you are fast dying. There is only one thing that can be done for you. Whatever gifts you have to friends or family—whatever messages you wish to send, give them to me. They shall be delivered, I promise."

"Friends?" echoed the dying man thickly. "Family?"

He broke into a stifled laugh which choked away to nothingness. His arms and legs twisted convulsively together. Then he lay still, looking up to the broad white face of the moon with dull eyes. He was dead!

"A plague has been removed from the world," said his grace of Ipswich, kneeling by the motionless body. "I call you all to witness that I have never yet read, or seen, or heard of such malice. Yet, now that he is gone, God rest him and give him peace in English ground."

So saying, he closed the eyes of the fencer. He raised the sword from the limp hand which could no longer hold it.

"And, my friends," continued the duke, "since he was a black-guard, but yet a matchless man with a sword, and since fencing is of all arts the most noble, it is fitting that no hand after his should manage this weapon. It was given to him, I believe, by a prince of the blood royal of Spain. Let it be buried with him."

With this he snapped the rapier across his knee, dropped the broken fragments upon the ground, and turned away.

CHAPTER XXXII

THE FOG BEGINS TO LIFT

WHAT CLOVELLY SAW when he wiped his sword blade and put it up in the sheath again was not the dead man on the ground, or the broken rapier; neither did he hear the words of the duke, except as a meaningless echo, for his whole mind was bent upon Cecily, his wife.

She no longer prayed, but leaning weakly against one of the pillars which made a portico on the west side of the little court; her head was fallen, and the steep shadow lay across her face. Clovelly took heed of this with a peculiar agony of spirit.

"Is it despair because her tormentor has conquered? Or is it utter thanksgiving because I have not fallen?"

These were the questions he asked himself, sadly. But in the meantime, his grace of Ipswich had taken possession of him and was dragging him into the house, pouring forth a jovial confession of his villainy covered slightly by a pretense of a mere sporting spirit:

"I was tired of hearing the Frenchman praised as the paragon of all earthly swordsmen. I made a bet with Ormonde that I could furnish an Englishman who would whip Lascelle to death in a fair fight, hand to hand, foot to foot, sword to sword.

"Ormonde was so confident that he offered me odds of three to one. But I disdained the taking of them, for I knew that you would be my champion, Clovelly! And I knew that an English hand and an English heart would match any in all the world."

In the meantime they had come close to Cecily, and the hand of the duke turned to iron on Clovelly's arm.

"By all that's holy," whispered his grace, "I had forgotten her! Present me."

And Clovelly, as he murmured the name of the great noble, and saw Ipswich sweep his finest bow to the girl, told himself that he had come to the end of the bitterest part that ever a man had been called upon to play. But there was still more before him; even crueller minutes to outface. The duke ushered them both into the house, and as they walked on, he found an opportunity to whisper in Clovelly's ear:

"Is she stout oak and willing to give truths a name?" he asked. "Or is she mincing with her words? Does she take greater care of herself in her talk than in her actions?"

"Your grace," muttered Clovelly guardedly, "she is a puzzle which I have not been able to solve. I have ridden with her on the road all these days, but I know less about her at this moment than when I first caught sight of her."

"That makes me think you a philosopher, Clovelly. It is usually in the twentieth year of a man's married life that he begins to find his wife extraordinary. But, you, Clovelly, are an exceptionally rare and lucky fellow. You have probed the nature of your wife to the bottom in half a fortnight—"

"My lord," said Clovelly, through his teeth, "no more talk about man and wife, if you please."

"What, man? Did you not really marry her?"

"Only with words—an empty ceremony."

"By Heavens, Clovelly, did you hire a false priest for the purpose? Have you gone to such a length as that?"

"No," Clovelly replied heavily. "We were married by a man of God—and I wedded her with a ring."

His jovial grace of Ipswich stared at his companion, and stared far harder with wonder when he heard the pirate muttering to himself: "What have I done? What have I done?"

"Hark, Clovelly!" whispered the duke. "Tell me, by all that's wonderful, have you a conscience in this matter?"

"What?" asked Clovelly, starting as though out of a dream.

"This little trickster of a pretty-faced girl—"

"You are right! You are a thousand times right. I thank your grace for recalling me to myself. No, no! I have no conscience in the matter, only knowing that in this way, and in this way alone, I shall be able to sail the Main again and do the work I have sworn to do there."

"Spoken like the true Clovelly of whom all London, I swear, talks half of every day."

"The ship is prepared for me, then?"

"She is ready—ballasted with a good cargo, manned by a selected gang of murderers, thieves, cheats, coiners, deserters, adventurers. They would storm the Tower of London for a shilling a man. You'll love them, Clovelly! And they have the clear presentment of their characters written at large in their faces."

"Good!" said Clovelly, but his voice somehow was weak.

So they came into a little room which, it was apparent, was part of the duke's peculiar quarters. It was no more than an alcove with some shelves of books, a fire burning to the side, a Persian carpet of tangled reds and blues and golds upon the floor; some monstrous dragons and other works in china, according to the newly introduced fashion, and, above all, a hanging lamp which was supported by a slender chain of gold and cast up, as it burned, a slender stream of vapor, which curled across the ceiling and then dropped into delicate rifts through the room which it filled with the most exquisite fragrance.

The central table, which was of ebony richly inlaid with ivory, was covered with a litter of papers at which his grace had just been working. He knocked them into a heap, sat lightly upon the edge of the table, swinging a foot, and waved Cecily and Michael Clovelly to chairs. Neither of them, however, moved,

Clovelly because he was deep in thought, and the girl because she was beginning to turn cold with fear.

"We have now come to the time for our agreement," said Ipswich in his pleasantest manner. "I presume you know, *madame,* that your husband is presently called away to duties in a very distant land, and that I am to serve as your protector during his absence?"

There was a frightened cry from Cecily, which brought a frown of surprise to the face of the duke and made Clovelly start.

"Michael," she demanded, "what does it mean?"

"I have promised," he answered, finding it hard to meet her great eyes, "to bring you to a heaven upon earth. And here it is. What will you have, Cecily? Great wealth, power, half the kingdom at your beck? It is common knowledge that his grace is the key to the king's heart, and you will have the turning of it."

"You have sold me!"

His grace stepped to the farther side of the chamber and waited, ill at ease at this unexpected turn of events, rubbing his chin with his finger tips and looking hastily from one face to the other. But Clovelly saw that his eye was kindling. And, indeed, Cecily had never seemed so lovely as she was now, with fear making her pale and despair giving her courage.

"Sold you?" echoed Clovelly, gloomily. "I have only done my best to advance you. What higher position could you ask?"

"To be your *wife,* Michael—your true wife to love you—to honor and obey you. Michael, Michael, you have sworn to protect me!"

And now light broke upon the mind of Michael Clovelly. He looked wildly about him upon the luxury of that room where a whole fortune had been lavished to make the comfort of a single corner of a house. He stared again at his grace of Ipswich.

The evidence of his eyes and of his ears had been against this woman, to damn her as one who loved pleasure only; but here was evidence almost equally strong that she preferred poverty with him to all that wealth could do for her.

"Your grace," he said, "we must talk further upon this matter."

"Let *madame* retire to the next room," said Ipswich, biting his lip.

He went to the door and opened it upon an adjoining chamber.

"No, no!" cried Cecily. "If I leave you, what may happen to me, God alone knows. Why should you talk to him?"

"There is no other way," said Michael, shaking his head.

Then he went to her and took her hand. And, as he stood close to her, she felt his whole body trembling with excitement.

"Can you trust me, Cecily?" he said.

She lifted her head at that, and looked him steadily, quietly, in the face. There is a strength and a courage needed to meet the weight of a man's eye, but strength and courage were in her. And this sad, unshrinking patience gave her beauty such a poignant grace that Clovelly's heart ached.

He could only say: "Wait in the next room beyond this door. You will not be long alone."

"Is it good-by, Michael?" she asked him quietly, and before he could answer she was gone through the door.

He closed the door upon her and turned to Ipswich, who was regarding him steadily beneath a scowl of anger.

"Mr. Clovelly," he said grimly, "I fear that the country has had an ill effect upon you. Or is it considered good manners even in the country to whisper before one's host?"

Clovelly flushed, but there was such a wealth of happiness crowding into his heart at that moment that he could not be angry.

"Your grace," he explained, "we must come to a new agreement."

"Ah!"

"I agreed to bring the lady to you."

"Exactly."

"And I have done so."

"In a manner—yes."

"And now, my lord, I shall take her away from you!"

"By the dear Heavens, Clovelly, you are mad to say so."

"Your grace," said Clovelly, "will hold me to my contract?"

"Strictly, Clovelly. I have seen her, man! I reached for gold, and I have found diamonds. Let her go again? I am not quite witless, my friend."

"My lord," Clovelly remarked, "I have in my time been a sufficient rascal. I have been a pirate, a swashbuckler, an outlawed highwayman, and do you think that I shall now hesitate to steal away the woman I love?

"I have fulfilled my contract, I tell you. I have brought her to your house. As for the ship which is your price, let it sail or sink for all of me. I want none of it.

"Only Cecily I desire, and her I shall have, by force, if need be. But surely your grace will not attempt to keep a woman who has shown that she has no liking for you!"

"For the moment, perhaps not," the duke admitted. "Her head, I see, has been turned by her galloping, ranting, fighting cavalier who has dragged her from her father's house and half across the kingdom. But that will pass. I know ways to soften stubborn hearts, Clovelly.

"No, no—for the matter of her present reluctance—it is a mere nothing.

"It is not to be considered. And as for taking her away with you again—tush, man, she has been bought and sold. I do not care to put a new price on her. As for taking her away by force—I tell you Clovelly, that I have a dozen men here, any two of whom could stop you."

These statements Clovelly seemed to consider for a time, leaning against the wall and looking down at the floor. But presently he stepped without a word to the door, turned the key in the lock, and dropped it in his pocket.

"You are quite right, sir," he said. "There is only one way in which I can safely take her away, and that is through your command."

"How will you buy that from me? Tell me, Clovelly? I warn you that I have taken a deeper fancy to her than to any trifle that has met my eyes these many years. For she has more than beauty, Clovelly. She has brains! The clever minx can play the part of virtue as well as any good woman I ever saw, and—"

"My lord, you are speaking of my wife!"

"Ten thousand devils, Clovelly! Are you mad?"

"You speak of prices and purchases. I can pay a great price, sir."

"Of pirate gold, Clovelly?" sneered the duke.

"Of pirate gold, my lord. Do you see?"

And, slipping his rapier from its sheath, he made it swerve so dexterously through the air that the yellow lamplight flashed solid upon it.

"Ah!" cried Ipswich. "Is that the tune? You will murder me to take the girl safely away with you?"

"If it is necessary," said Clovelly calmly, "I shall stab you to the heart, my lord, and take my wife away with me."

His grace turned crimson with anger. His rapier hissed and hummed in the air; he brought it forth with so much violence. Then he saluted Clovelly deliberately.

"You are already half-spent with fighting Lascelle," he observed. "Do you deliberately challenge me in spite of that?"

"In the name of God," said Clovelly, "begin!"

"She is worth the price!" cried his grace, as if the picture of her beauty had at that instant flashed more brightly across his memory. "Clovelly, you are right. Gold cannot buy a woman. The metal is too base. The steel alone is worthy of her. On guard!"

He gasped out the last word as he lunged with fury. His sword was flicked away with a touch of the other blade so soft that it was like the pressure of a bare hand. And the duke suddenly was aware that it was one thing to see Clovelly fence—it was quite another to feel his opposition.

A thousand light, quick hands seemed to surround Clovelly and pushed danger gently away from him. For a moment he stood on the defense. Then he began to attack.

His grace was a brave man, a thousand times proved. Moreover, he was an exquisite fencer who fought like an artist of infinite invention. To the very last he would be dangerous.

But against the rush of Clovelly's attack, against that onslaught of a dozen schools of fence, he was carried back as a log before a tide. Through the door of the study and into the larger chamber beyond he retreated, where the clicking of steel on steel sounded smaller and colder and raised many little echoes from the walls.

Still he kept a good front while his breath held, but when his wind was gone he was helpless. The point of Clovelly's rapier flickered before his eyes.

"Your grace," gasped Clovelly, "let us make an end. You see that the advantage is in my hand, but God forbid that I should use it—"

"Damn your courtesy," said the nobleman hotly. "I am as ready to die now as a year hence!"

And with this, he rushed blindly in upon Clovelly. The latter might have killed him three times during that blind advance, but instead, he chose to glide out of the way, dancing back until Ipswich should come to his senses.

Then fate took a hand against the conqueror. Clovelly's foot lodged on a small rug which slipped from beneath him as if the floor had been greased. He landed heavily upon his side, his wrist striking so solidly that the nerves were numbed, the rapier clattered from his fingers, and he lay prostrate and helpless before his enemy.

It appeared for an instant that Ipswich would pass his weapon through the body of his opponent. He leaned above him with his face swollen and reddened by exertion, his sword quivering in his hand.

"Surrender, Clovelly!" he commanded.

"The devil has played on your side," answered Clovelly. "Do with me what you will. I shall not surrender."

"You are in my hands."

"Stab and be damned!"

CHAPTER XXXIII

AN UNENDURABLE DOUBT

HIS GRACE WAS often cruel, but never wantonly so. Now he shook his head.

"If you were any other man in England," he said at last, "I'd send the blade through you, Clovelly. But I've an idea that you are a man of honor, my friend. Rise!"

Clovelly stood up, white-lipped from the shame of his defeat, almost the first that had ever come to him sword in hand.

"Tush, man, tush!" said Ipswich. "You act as though some fat old man had beaten you, or some boy newly come into his swordship and his oaths. But I tell you, man, that no man living can say that he has seen Ipswich worsted with the small sword.

"Matters went a bit against me at first; my wind is short and I'm damnably out of practice. But aside from that, and the bit of bad luck which brought you a fall, I think I should have paid you home before the end."

Thus spoke the duke, raising his spirits as he argued more with himself than with the other. He had been a desperate and half-beaten man a moment before, shamed and helpless before the swordsmanship of Clovelly.

But now, as he talked of the battle, he smoothed out the doubt from his brain. He was laying the basis for a magnificent lie, concerning that battle, which would be bruited through the fashionable circles of London the next day. And as he thought how much that tale would do to establish him as an Achilles as well as a Paris, he could not help looking upon his associate with a greater warmth of good feeling. At least, Clovelly made no reply and his silence might be interpreted as an agreement.

"However," continued his grace, "I have no desire to use my sword to make my fortune—or to save it, even! We have fought for the lady fairly and honorably.

"Chance and the sword gives her to me. I might make no other payment. But instead, I shall carry out to the letter my first agreement with you.

"The ship is prepared. You may take command of it when you will. And that should prudently be as soon as possible, for the king's men are looking for you, Clovelly. Old Hampton has put another five hundred pounds on top of his standing reward to any one who will bring about your capture—or your death!"

"There is only one thing in the world which is of any concern to me," said Clovelly.

"The Spanish Main! Of course! To a man of your metal, there must be action. England is a dull place. By gad, I feel it myself every day. Only dull habit makes a fool of me and keeps me here."

"Not the Spanish Main. There is only my wife, my lord."

Ipswich made a wry face.

"You love her, Clovelly?"

The husband shrugged his shoulders.

"But how under heaven you can," said the duke, "is a miracle to me. You are a man of pride. And you have seen with your own eyes and heard with your own ears enough to—"

Clovelly groaned.

And at this, his grace drew back a little and looked at Clovelly with new eyes.

"This is the way of it, then," he nodded, speaking more to himself than to Clovelly. "The tale of Samson and Delilah over again "

Clovelly was silent.

"Take up your sword!" said Ipswich suddenly.

Clovelly's eyes gleamed. Then, with a sigh, he murmured: "Will you run that risk again, my lord?"

His grace smiled faintly.

"I have nothing to fear from that damned subtle blade of yours," he declared. "You are an honest man, Clovelly. You are a thousand times more honest than you yourself guess, and I have nothing to fear from you. That sword will be locked into the sheath until I give it permission to be drawn."

Clovelly stooped without a word and replaced the weapon in its scabbard.

"Now, my friend, I can offer you a fair gambler's chance."

"My lord?"

"The Spanish Main, to which a vow leads you, has shrunk to a small pond, I take it."

"There is more treasure in one word from her than in a thousand galleons, your grace."

"Poetically expressed. Very much to the point. But concerning another matter: If you should attempt to live with her as man with wife, consider that you are also marrying your doubt of her."

"God knows it!"

"You will put only one meaning upon the smiles of men you pass in the street."

"I shall endure it."

"You think so now. But I tell you, Clovelly, you are wedding yourself to an infinite torment whose fire shall not cease to burn if you live five score years."

"It is true," groaned Clovelly.

"In spite of all this, you will have her?"

"If God will help me to her."

"Now, Clovelly, your doubt of her was based chiefly upon a story told by one man."

"Talk of Marberry—and the evidence of my own eyes!"

"Eyes and ears will lie. I say, pull your cloak about your face and go to Marberry. Wring the full truth from him. If it is as black as I think you will find it, then I am trusting that you will never wish to lay eyes on the lady again. But if you make that rascal confess that he has lied, then your doubt vanishes like a pricked bubble!"

Clovelly raised his head with a start.

"And while I am gone—the lady—"

"Remains here with me."

"My lord?"

"I have said it! She remains here with me. While you work in your own way, I work in mine. When you return, even if you wish to have her, I trust that I shall have persuaded her that there is happiness with Ipswich."

Clovelly turned pale.

"Only persuasion will be used, on my honor! And I'll wager you a hundred pounds, Clovelly—"

"My lord, on this subject I do not bet."

"Your answer, then?"

"There is only one choice for me. I must take it, and leave her here—God defend the right!"

"You have grown into a pious pirate, Clovelly. But now, start on to your work. Adieu!"

"Adieu, my lord."

"You have ways of making the fellow speak even against his will?"

A smile of infinitely cruel malignity appeared upon the grim face of Michael Clovelly. Then, gathering his cloak about him, he retreated to the door, bowed, and disappeared. His grace stepped to a bellcord and pulled it, whereat the soft-footed Randal instantly appeared. At sight of the crumpled, displaced rugs, an overturned chair, and the disorder of his master's person, his eyes grew big.

"Say nothing; guess nothing, Randal," commanded the master. "To-day I have mastered the finest blade in the world, fighting upon equal terms. Bring me a glass of sherry. Then lay out that newest suit of plum-colored velvet. Quickly! Quickly! I have a great campaign to make!"

CHAPTER XXXIV

GOSSIP

THERE WAS NEED for the porter who worked in the service of Edward Marberry to be a man of discretion and of perception. He gave the young gentleman who wished to see his master so importunately one glance and was about to close the door and shut the fellow into the outer dark when something caught his eyes—of sufficient importance to make him open again, hastily, and stare at the man outside. He now seemed to make sure, for suddenly he began to smile more with his eyes than his lips and stepped back, waving to the stranger to enter.

The later slipped with a light step within the door, a slender figure, rain-beaten, with a cloak of black which time had rusted, a hat with a bedraggled feather, and boots enriched with red mud half way to the knees.

"I'm sure," said the porter, "that Mr. Marberry will see you—sir."

And with an odd accent upon the last word, he left his guest and disappeared into his master's room. He came again with his smile now broad enough to be plainly visible. And he ushered the nameless stranger into a high-ceilinged room at one end of which was a table covered with various bottles and several glasses. Beside the table, resting in a great reclining chair, heaped with pillows, was the invalid who had been recruiting himself and killing the time with recourse to the wine-bottle.

It was Edward Marberry himself, not yet recovered from a wound which he had received at sword play with Clovelly not many days before. Suffering of the flesh had been less than the suffering of the spirit of this man, who could not bear to be shut away from all of his old delights of fluttering around the court, of haunting the fashionable coffee-houses, of hearing a rare word from a wit here, and a profound judgment there; of sipping like a bee at a thousand flowers, a thousand bits of gossip spiced with malice, and blending all that pollen into a honey of delicious lies to be given freely away to those who were his friends.

How could Ned Marberry endure a life cooped within half a dozen rooms? No matter that his friends came often about him. The aroma of the tales they told him was staled already by time. For what is the joy of sitting still like an old woman over her knitting and listening to the chattered scandal which two granddaughters rattle for each other and for her ears?

Far sweeter, far sweeter, surely, to overhear a conversation whispered in a corner of Will's coffee-house with so keen an ear that all the double meanings are deciphered and unspoken things are added to the spoken. How exquisite a delight to probe through the conversation of two fops and under the flowing of their banter to discover the very names of the ladies of whom they talk!

In such arts was Marberry a master. He was, indeed, a known genius in his line and those who wished not for the rank and open talk of the court but for those hidden undercurrents and for those overtones of mischief, hunted him out and made much of him, if perchance he would open his budget of news.

For although it was known that he would rather invent lies than be discovered without what he reported to be a "new tale," yet his lies were so cunningly planned and always based at the foundation upon such bedrock of truth, that they never failed to come near enough to the truth to make some beauty in Whitehall turn pale or some gentleman at a fashionable tavern wince while the steel glided through his spirit.

But having been confined to his room, or damned to it, as

he phrased his imprisonment, every hour and every day infinitely increased his misery and he was now in a poisonous frame
of mind so that a smile of nervous malice was constantly upon
his thin lips and wrinkling his haggard cheeks, and his tongue
carried a mortal sting in every sentence.

He watched the shadow of the closing door before he looked
up from his chair toward his visitor. Although the face of the
stranger was thoroughly masked by a high furling cloak collar,
yet Marberry saw enough to make him shrug his shoulders and
laugh.

"You've ridden through the mud, then," he said. "Lord, Betty,
you've come on a far journey like a little fool. Don't stand there
like an idiot with your face still masked. Come, come!

"Any man with an eye in his head could tell by the mincing
manner in which you stand with your feet so close together,
that there is a woman beneath that cloak, and a damned silly
one, I believe! But show your face, minx! I'm tired of talking to
a wall."

At this, the collar of the cloak was lowered.

"By all the dear heavens!" breathed the voluptuary, half rising
himself from his chair until the sudden burning of his wound
made him release his hold upon the arms of the chair and sink
back again.

Then: "Clovelly!" shouted Marberry.

"A little louder," sneered Clovelly. "London will be glad to
hear that I am come."

"Have you dared to show your face in the city?" cried Marberry. "When the whole town is placarded with descriptions of
you and rewards offered?"

"I have brought some few along with me," said Clovelly.

He plucked some crumpled handbills out of his pocket and
cast them upon the table.

"The price of my head goes up," he observed casually. "What
with the contributions of the worthy squire and my lord Pennistone, I considered that there was enough offered to make

me a fat prize even to a prince of the blood royal, but now in comes the solid Puritan, Oliver Perth, and claps a round two hundred pounds upon my head in addition. 'Slife, Mr. Marberry, this is a forwarding of the king's justice with a vengeance, eh?"

Marberry gazed upon him, fascinated.

"But what brings you to me?" he asked. "Why are you come to me, rather than to any other in London?"

"Partly," said Clovelly, "to confer a favor, and partly to receive one."

"And the nature of these favors?"

"Why, Marberry, I confer a favor upon you by giving you a subject for gossip. Am I wrong? Half of London will flock to your chambers when they learn that the celebrated man-killer and robber, Michael Clovelly, actually presumed to call upon you and tell you anecdotes of the open road."

"But what anecdotes will you tell, Clovelly?"

"I should not presume to put words into the mouth of a master. I abandon such a small matter entirely to the invention of Mr. Marberry."

"You are kind," Marberry declared, smiling in spite of himself.

"But," said Clovelly, "do not have me kill too many men. I detest bloodshed, on my honor. Six or ten you may reasonably put in, but there call a halt. You may tell them, also, that Clovelly drank your health in your own wine."

Here he poured a glass of sherry from the bottle which was standing on the table, tasted it cautiously, rolled it in his mouth until he had formed an opinion of its excellence, and then drank off the rest of the glass as slowly and as luxuriously as a cat finishing a plate of cream.

"Will it serve?" asked Marberry.

"It is good. It is at least good enough. I have tasted some sherry lately that was like a mixture of plum juice and fire combined. You are a lucky fellow, Marberry, to have such wine under your roof."

"I am very sensible of that. But since we seem to have finished with the favor which you are doing me, what is the favor which I may do for you?"

"A simple one, but one of the greatest importance. You must know that every true highwayman, Marberry, warms his heart in his constant isolation and loneliness by reflecting that most of the world is constantly talking about him. All lonely men are vain you know.

"And what you may do for me, is simply to repeat the details of my visit to you with a few embroideries from your fancy—just such as you think will furnish a good tale. Thus we are both benefited."

"Clovelly, this is all beside the point. You have come to London—"

"To hear the talk about myself. I have been loitering through the streets of London all day tasting the gossip and picking up odds and ends of information about myself, and above all enjoying the safety."

"If you were seen?"

"I shall not be, simply because people see only what they expect to see, and because they are blind to the unexpected. I could walk through London for a month before the hue and the cry would be raised against me. When I had heard what I could in the nooks and the corners, I decided to come to you so that my call might serve to give you a basis for invention."

"It is true!" murmured Marberry. "His grace of Ipswich will forget that he and I have fallen out and will come to hear the odd tale from my own lips."

"I have no doubt but that you will make a very good thing of this visit."

"It is a treasure, Clovelly. I forgive you the thrust that chained me here. I am your friend."

"You are very kind, sir."

"But now to come a little closer to the cold facts of your

call—you are out of money, Clovelly. You have come here seeking a little cash?"

"Nonsense. When there are so many fat wallets in London one does one's begging with the edge of a knife; it cuts the strings of purses painlessly."

At this though, he burst into a soft chuckling. But all this while his glance never wavered from the eyes of his host, and though he laughed, his expression grew not a whit more pleasant. This was uneasily observed by Marberry, yet he forced himself to laugh in company with his strange guest.

"You are rare, Clovelly."

"And yet, Marberry, I confess that there is another reason for my coming to you—keep your hand from that bellcord, my friend! Good! While I stand here chatting, you are thinking what an excellent figure I would make upon the scaffold beside Jack Ketch. Are you not?"

"In the name of heaven, do you think me such a brute as this?"

But he could not constrain his blush.

"Enough, Marberry. We know each other."

"Then—be damned to you for a knave. What will you have?"

"The truth about a very small matter—a matter as small as a woman, in fact; and her name is *Madame Clovelly*."

CHAPTER XXXV

DARKNESS FLEES

MARBERRY WAVED HIS hand as one who will take up a conversation only by compulsion, so to speak.

"Women, at best, are poor things for talk, Clovelly," said he.

Clovelly sat down lightly on the broad arm of a chair and swung one foot in the air as he continued: "You are a known man, Marberry. Not a man or a woman in London but knows what a clever devil you are with the ladies. They cannot resist you, man."

The other smiled in spite of himself.

"No talk of that," he remarked carelessly.

"But it must be talked of when all London is willing to listen and to believe. But, Marberry, I was with Milverton, as I think you know, on a certain night when we saw you leave a certain garden, which shall be nameless."

"I remember," growled Marberry. "And the next morning Milverton would walk with me. I peppered him properly and then in come you with your damned sword magic and run me through!

"By the eternal heavens, Clovelly, it is neither right nor fair for such fellows as yourself to take the field against simple, honest gentlemen. What chance have we against you? No more chance than a man off the streets has to match the tricks of a master juggler."

He shuddered as he remembered.

"If I had known about you then what I know now," he said,

"I'd have seen you damned before I'd have engaged you. I'd have set a gang of bullies to maul you in the streets by night to keep off the meeting!"

He shivered again. "Pour me another glass of that sherry, Clovelly. I'm cold through and through when I even think of it. You might have killed me on the spot—with no more effort upon your part. Gad, there was a life—a special malice in that sword of yours. I swear to heaven that it worked against me of its own account and of its own accord."

"You say much too much, sir. But concerning the lady—for, you see, I did *not* kill you."

"What about the lady? What about the lady?" asked Marberry sharply. "What the devil have you to learn from me about the lady? You're married to her, aren't you?"

"After a fashion of speaking, I am."

"After a fashion? After a fashion? What mean you by that?"

"You are testy, Mr. Marberry, but the question I wish to ask may be very shortly put."

"Put it then, put it then, and be damned. I'm tired of this talk, Clovelly."

"In one word, then, was Milverton right?"

"About what? No, damn him, he's never right."

"Ah!"

"One would think that I had given you a present of a great estate to judge by your face. What is it you want to know of me?"

"You have already answered me when you said that Milverton was wrong in thinking that Cecily Medhurst had been your mistress."

"Did I say that, then? Well!"

"Is it not true, man?"

"You are very pale, Clovelly."

"Is it true, Marberry?"

" 'Fore God, one would think that you loved the girl."

"No matter for all that. You destroy my very soul by refusing to speak. Say yes or no!"

"To what?"

"Marberry, if you push me too far, remember that I am a man of violence, and I have been in places where sick men had scant grace."

"Come, lad, I only teased you. It's about Cecily, is it? But you cannot come to me expecting to pull out all the secrets of my inward life like a soul-doctor to whom I'm confessing my sins."

"I have not expected it for nothing. Look here, my friend. Look here!"

He drew his hand from his pocket and clapped upon the table beside Marberry a long, almond-shaped emerald. The other took it up with a cry and looked to it with a keen and knowing eye.

"Very good, upon my word!" he declared. "This will do, indeed, Clovelly. This is a very precious jewel or else I am a blind owl. No, by the Lord, if this green heaven came near me, the blindness would leave my eyes to let me see it. And this is an exquisite and a perfect jewel, my friend. What the devil do you mean with it?"

"It's the price, my friend. It's the price I'm paying you for one bit of that truth drawn from your inner life. Tell me: Were you the messenger of Oliver Perth, only, or were you in truth in that garden on a mission of your own?"

The face of the roué wrinkled to a smile.

"Very good!" he murmured. "Very good, indeed! Of course, I was there simply as the messenger of the Roundhead."

"Marberry, you smile."

"I cannot help but smile—when I think that I was only the messenger of Perth."

Clovelly staggered, and dropped his hand upon the back of a chair to support himself.

"It is true, then," he whispered. "And she is as black as I have guessed!"

Marberry shrugged his shoulders and cherished the emerald between his hands.

"For such a price—one must tell the truth even about a charming lady, my friend. Even though the truth is a fire that burns you."

Then, brighter than the shining of the jewel, the blue-white of the naked sword blade shone in Clovelly's hand.

"What a good work it would be," he snarled through his set teeth, "to loose that jackal soul of yours and send it hunting in another world than this! What an act of charity it would be!"

Marberry shrank from him and twisted both his hands into a knot before his face to keep from his view the quivering, bright death.

"Do you mean to murder me, Clovelly, for telling the truth?"

"No. But for most damnably lying! You have two seconds in which you may commend yourself to God—if you have a God! Marberry, you are about to die."

"No!" screamed the wounded man, cowering in the chair, his lips grinning in the agony of his fear. "In the name of mercy, Clovelly."

"Speak the truth, then!"

"I shall—I shall—"

He choked and gibbered in his frantic effort to speak, while the terror nearly froze his lips.

"Now!" commanded Clovelly.

"I came from Perth to her!" gasped Marberry.

"Is that the truth?"

"The whole truth."

"You lied when you hinted that she served you as a mistress?"

"I lied, Clovelly."

"To make the world think you invincible with women?"

"Yes—yes—before God, you shame me. But that was the reason."

"And you sacrificed the pure name of a blameless girl for that same reason?"

"I confess it."

"Tell me this—have you ever dreamed or guessed at evil in her?"

"No!" gasped Marberry, twisting in his chair as the foulness of his sin was drawn out from him in its full horror. "I swear to you, Clovelly, that so far as I have known her, she has always been more of a saint than a woman."

There broke from Clovelly's lips a wild shout of joy. He cast up his hands, his face suffused with color.

"Then instinct was right," he cried. "It has told me the truth whenever I have been near her. It has roared out to me above the evidence of my eyes and my ears. She had met you secretly for the sake of Perth. With the courage and the pure heart of a blameless girl, she dared to interview you in the middle of the night and dismiss you herself from the gate of the garden."

"She did."

"Marberry—you consummate devil! Oh, Cecily, my beautiful—"

And he turned and rushed from the room.

When he was gone, Marberry reached for the bell—but a second thought made him draw back his hand again. Whatever he had lost in that interview, he had gained a jewel of which a king might have been proud.

He leaned back in his chair again. The congested look of fear and shame left his face. The emerald lay like a pool of the purest beauty in the palm of his hand. It was more to this voluptuary than any woman.

But in the meantime, Clovelly had reached the street with a brain on fire. For the dread which haunted him now was that at the very moment when he discovered the perfect purity of Cecily, she would be lost to him.

It was strange enough, he thought, that she could have preferred him to Ipswich even for an instant. But it would be a miracle indeed if she still preferred him to the duke when the latter had had a chance to show himself in his most winning fashion to her and display before her all the resources of his fortune, all the talents of his person.

It was White Harry that he rode through the streets of London, but even the speed of this powerful animal was slower than a snail's pace dragging him wearily out the Oxford road. White Harry was staggering with exhaustion when his master at last flung himself from the saddle.

Into the court ran Clovelly; and there the solid blackness struck him in the face. No light was burning. All was sordid darkness.

It so sickened him that he felt his strength give way at the knees. He staggered to the nearest door. The handle turned at once and admitted him to a pitch-dark hall. He called out he knew not what, and the long echoes rolled away. The house was empty.

And then, feeling what it meant—that Cecily had indeed made her choice and that Ipswich had taken her with him to another dwelling—all his agony broke from him in a terrible cry: "Cecily!"

He dropped upon his knees; he covered his face with his hands; no tears came from his eyes, but his body shivered and was wrenched with agony. For this, he told himself mutely, was the judgment of God come upon him. Here was the end of his strength. Here was a defeat which all his skill with the sword could not redeem, but he was wrecked as utterly as a fine ship struck suddenly upon a reef.

Then it seemed to Clovelly that he heard that voice of infinite sweetness calling to him out of the distance of his memory, "Michael!" as she had called on that other night when he had lost her in the wood, and she had guided him back to her with her own voice. At that memory, he felt he should go mad.

And ah! what a consummate fool he had been to doubt her

after that final proof of faith. What a fool to make the slightest question of her, after once looking into the crystal purity of her eyes!

But, small and far, yet vibrant with grief and fear, he heard that cry again: "Michael!"

"It is not possible!" groaned Clovelly. "God, having seen me and judged me, would not let me find her again. This is all an illusion to drive me mad."

A door opened, and into the thick blackness of that hall came her very voice like a blinding light to Clovelly:

"Michael!"

He tried to answer, but his throat was aching and stiff with the marvel of this thing. Then he stretched out his arms, although he could not rise from his knees.

He managed to utter a sound, he knew not what word, but it brought a wailing cry of joy down through the darkness toward him, until suddenly she was within his arms, she was kneeling before him, she was weeping, and the catch and the panting of her breath stirred against his cheek.

"I have heard everything from that dog, Marberry," he told her. "I know it all—I know everything of your sweetness and goodness—of my blindness—"

"And I, Michael, know only this—which is that I love you, I love you, my dearest—"

AFTERWARD, they could speak of lesser things; they could descend out of the sweetness of their lovers' heaven to the dull and foolish earth and light a taper to aid their eyes. And then she gave him a letter which Ipswich had left with her for her husband when he came. He tore it open and read within:

> CLOVELLY:
> I have made your peace with the king. You are no longer an outlawed man. There is only one punishment for having doubted the blessed angel who has been foolish enough to love any man—that is to find her in a dark house alone. In the

meantime, know that that house is yours and everything in it. You will see that if I sometimes pay much for the services of a crafty man and an evil woman, I shall pay much more for the friendship of a strong man and a good woman. God bless you both with happiness. She is a dear child. I blush for my folly that I should have dared to doubt her.

The scoundrel Marberry must be left to me.

G.I.

When they had read that letter, they blew out the taper and sat silently in the darkness again, watching the moon rise over the woodland and then pass into the fragrant gloom of the chamber where they sat, creeping across the floor until their feet were bathed in silver, and the tendrils of the vine which swung at the window were little branches of purest silver also.

ABOUT THE AUTHOR

MAX BRAND IS a Californian who saw the West first in the central valley of the State, where the Coast Range ran low on one side and the Sierra Nevadas on clear days were green and brown over the foothills, and blue or glass-white above. He learned something of cattle and cattlemen among the great grasslands of the foothills, but he never was so deep in that Old West which is a golden legend to-day, as when he spent a few weeks with two old trappers near the Diablo Mountains, close to El Paso, in Texas.

Nick and Alec had fought Indians, ridden range, prospected for gold, made fortunes for others, and had never been able to spend all the wealth that had poured in upon their minds. Some of the glory of mountains and desert remained with them as a perpetual heritage. Nick, at seventy-eight, had a body bent and twisted by age; Alec at eighty was straight as a stick, with no visible sign of the passage of time about him. But Alec was apt to blame his inability to read upon a defect of his eyes.

They quarreled constantly. To Max Brand, Nick reported that Alec was just a touchy old idiot—who could not even read! And what is a man capable of when he cannot read print? Alec, with equal fervor, reported that poor Nick was not to be blamed for weakness of temper and mind, for, said Alec, when a man's body is bent his brain is sure to sag also! But in spite of their wrangling, the two loved one another with a perfect devotion. And the long tales which they told in the evenings, making

sixty years of Western history breathe
and repainting mountains and deserts,
have never been out of the mind of
Max Brand. Nothing is more vivid to
him than the memory of the little
shanty near the "tank," the small
stretchers on which the skins of coyotes
and bobcats were drying, and the
wrangling voices of old Nick and Alec.

Max Brand

Max Brand has been a traveler for
a great many years, from the Pacific
Islands to the deserts of northern Africa, but when he search-
es for stories, he most often goes back to that shanty in Texas,
and the voices of the two old men pour up in his mind. That is
why Western themes generally have come off his typewriter
during the last sixteen years. In fact, he has written more
Western stories than any other author. He is forty years old,
was born on the Coast, spent twenty-three years in California,
and since that time has lived east and west in diverse parts of
the world.

THE ARGOSY LIBRARY ™

SERIES 3 INCLUDES:

* BURROUGHS * ZAGAT * MERRITT *

* BRAND * KLINE *

* BEYER * HENDRYX *

* WIRT * VANARDY *

* WORTS *

THE BEST FICTION
FROM THE FRANK
A. MUNSEY LINE

TARZAN
AND THE JEWELS
OF OPAR
BY ARGOSY'S GREATEST AUTHOR
EDGAR RICE BURROUGHS®

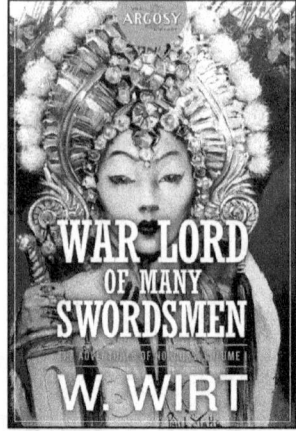

WAR LORD
OF MANY
SWORDSMEN
W. WIRT

CLOVELLY
BY WORLD FAMOUS AUTHOR
MAX BRAND

DRINK
WE DEEP
THE SCIENCE FICTION CLASSIC
ARTHUR LEO ZAGAT

THE GUN-
BRAND
BY NORTHWEST FICTION LEGEND
JAMES B. HENDRYX

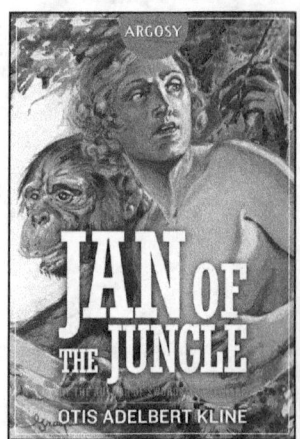

JAN OF
THE JUNGLE
OTIS ADELBERT KLINE

THE BLUE
FIRE PEARL
THE COMPLETE ADVENTURES OF SINGAPORE SAMMY VOLUME 1
GEORGE F. WORTS

THE MOON
POOL
& THE CONQUEST OF
THE MOON POOL
BY THE INSPIRATION FOR H.P. LOVECRAFT
ABRAHAM MERRITT

MINIONS
OF THE
MOON
THE SCIENCE FICTION CLASSIC
WILLIAM GREY BEYER

ALIAS THE
NIGHT WIND
BY THE CREATOR OF NICK CARTER
VARICK VANARDY

www.ingramcontent.com/pod-product-compliance
Lightning Source LLC
Chambersburg PA
CBHW071834020726
47502CB00004B/1349